LIONEL'S LEAP OF FAITH

Horses Heal Hearts Series Book Three

KIMBERLY BECKETT

---

1.   http://www.kimberlybeckett.com

Prologue

Lionel Hayes nervously paced the aisle of the stabling area of the Olympia International Horse Show in London. His horse, a leggy chestnut thoroughbred gelding named Accolade, was watching Lionel from his stall, and quickly appeared to pick up on Lionel's nervous energy. The gelding began to pace his stall, channeling his rider's tension. Lionel noticed Accolade's reaction, and, realizing he was the cause of the gelding's sudden change in behavior, stopped his pacing and forced himself to calm.

He took two deep breaths, focused his attention on the air flowing into and out of his lungs, and cleared his mind of any thoughts other than those of himself and the horse who had been there for him without fail from the moment Lionel discovered him at an out of the way racetrack in North Yorkshire. When he felt he had his emotions under control, Lionel approached the gelding, who had also stopped pacing. Accolade nickered at the man who had been the center of his life, his caretaker, trainer, and companion for the past seven years.

Lionel looked into the gelding's soft brown eyes. "I know you don't understand my worries, old man," Lionel said as he absently stroked his nose. "I'm sure you were giving me everything you had in our test today, but I noticed you were favoring the left front leg you injured a few weeks ago," Lionel sighed. Yes, the limp was slight, so slight that he was probably the only one who really noticed it, but this show would determine who would be selected for the British Olympic Dressage team, and Lionel couldn't afford to take any chances. This was his last opportunity to solidify his position as a selectee.

Maybe if he were a better rider, he could dazzle the judges and maneuver Accolade through the required movements without putting too much pressure on the weakened leg, but he had no confidence in his abilities while under the pressure of this high level of competition.

Accolade was a talented off-the-track thoroughbred that Lionel had trained with the help of his partner and lover, Nigel Crawford. Lionel and Nigel shared ownership of a business that took off-the-track thoroughbreds and rehabilitated them so they could be used as pleasure horses.

When Lionel brought Accolade home, Nigel immediately agreed with Lionel's assessment that this horse was special, and the two of them together spent many hours working with and training Accolade to the highest levels of dressage in just a few short years. The last thing Lionel wanted to do was let Nigel down. He had been so supportive of their efforts.

This lameness issue had raised its head weeks ago when Accolade came in from turnout limping. The vet had immediately been called, and diagnosed a deep bruise, probably caused by a kick from another horse. Not an uncommon injury, but the timing couldn't have been worse.

Knowing he had no choice, Lionel gave Accolade some time off to recuperate, and once the swelling had subsided, all had seemed fine. Accolade had been doing great, but after a few less than stellar training sessions, there was still some residual lameness in his left front leg that wasn't responding to the approved methods of treating inflammation. Lionel sighed. He knew the only sure-fire way to treat Accolade's lameness was to use a steroid currently on the banned substance list.

If he used the drug and was caught, he would be banned from the sport, potentially for life. If he didn't, and Accolade's lameness impaired his performance, he would forfeit his only chance to compete in the Olympic Games for Britain. Accolade would be denied the recognition he deserved, and he would lose the opportunity to bring a great deal of publicity to his and Nigel's business. Just at that moment, Accolade nickered at Lionel softly, then gently nudged him with his nose, as if urging him to decide.

"I know, boy. You're right. If I'm going to do something, I'd best be getting on with it." Lionel took a deep breath, his countenance one of resolve.

"I have one syringe left of the drug Dr. Caldwell gave me when you were first injured," Lionel told the horse. "If I'm lucky, I can give this to you now, you will be able to perform without pain, and no one will be the wiser. It's not fair that your talent is impaired because of a freak accident. You deserve to have the world see you at your best."

Lionel left Accolade to walk to the tack room then looked up and down the aisles to ensure no one was around to see him. He opened his tack trunk and unwrapped the syringe he had carefully packed as a last resort. It appeared the time had come to use it. His hand trembled slightly, and he took a deep breath to calm his already-frazzled nerves. *Get a grip, man, you know what you must do.* He took the medication, retraced his steps back down the stable aisle, and entered Accolade's stall to inject him.

As he approached Accolade, his heart rate quickened, and all his senses sharpened. Were those footsteps he heard in the distance? No, not possible. No one came out to the stables at this hour of the night.

Accolade again picked up on Lionel's tension and pawed the ground impatiently. It was as if he was telling Lionel to get on with it. *Do whatever you have to do and release this unbearable tension.* Lionel attempted to soothe the gelding by speaking softly. He took another deep breath and exhaled while quickly administering the injection.

"Lionel, what the hell are you doing?" A familiar voice demanded.

Lionel practically jumped out of his skin. His worst fear had come true. Not only had he been discovered, but the man who discovered him was Michael Stafford, his best friend from childhood. When they were both attending public school in Brighton, Michael had seen Lionel's desperation as a gay adolescent looking for meaning in his life and introduced him to horses. That one act of kindness had changed Lionel's life forever.

Today, however, Michael was a fellow competitor for a spot on the British Olympic dressage team. In fact, Michael wasn't just another competitor. It was common knowledge among those competing here this week that Michael Stafford and his black stallion Romeo were a shoo-in to make the team. In fact, they were the odds-on favorites to win the gold medal.

When Lionel finally got his heart rate back to a semblance of normal, he replied, "Nothing, Michael. Accolade seemed to be a bit off this afternoon in training, and I just came by to give him an anti-inflammatory."

Michael cast him a skeptical look. "There are very few anti-inflammatories that aren't banned for international competition. What is it you're using?"

"It's just something my home vet recommended for inflammation."

"You need to clear anything like that with the Team vet, you know that. I'll call him right away. You don't want to get in trouble for something like this."

Lionel's heart sank to his toes. "No, Michael, please. You're my best friend. Please don't do this." Lionel's voice was choked with desperation and fear.

A flash of sympathy crossed Michael's visage, but was quickly followed by a cold, detached glare. "I don't know what you're up to, Lionel, but you jeopardize all our chances if you make the Team and you're doing something illegal. I've got to call the vet."

Without hesitation, Michael did just that, and subsequent testing confirmed that the steroid Lionel had used was indeed banned. Lionel and Accolade were ejected from the trials and any hope of competing in the Olympic Games.

Word of his disgrace made it to the press, of course, and Lionel's reputation was ruined. For several months, many dressage, eventing, and hunter/jumper trainers who would have routinely bought potential buyers to Lionel and Nigel's farm as a source for a well-trained pleasure mount bypassed their farm for other suppliers. After a time, Nigel, who had been born with a weak heart, found his condition worsening due in large part to the stress of fighting to maintain a floundering business. Less than a year after Lionel's fall from grace, Lionel watched helplessly as the love of his life slowly passed away.

Although Lionel had initially blamed Michael Stafford's betrayal for his misfortunes, Lionel eventually accepted that he and he alone had made the decision to give Accolade the prohibited drug, and that he alone should pay the consequences.

Nonetheless, Lionel was determined to fulfill the purpose for which he and Nigel had originally started Second Chance Farm — finding and rehabilitating off-the- track racehorses and other horses that had been subjected to abuse so that they might find a second chance at a happy productive life. So, with Nigel's memory to guide him and provide him courage, he resolved to do just that.

Chapter 1

Two years after the Olympic Trials — Present day

"Yes, Randall." Lionel Hayes put his hand over his cell phone mic, looked over at his barn manager, Rachel Adams, sighed dramatically, and rolled his eyes. Rachel grinned back at him and winked. Lionel returned his attention to the phone. "I know you've been sending me your best riders, but Gideon's Rainbow is not just any horse. He will need a rider who has just the right combination of supreme confidence, sensitivity, and common sense to be successful. If the rider lacks any one of those qualities, the match won't work."

"I understand your frustration, Lionel," said Randall Bridges, the UK Equestrian Team Director for the Jumper Division. "But Montgomery Campbell is not like any of the riders you've ever seen. I've watched him, and he's something special. He's proven himself time and again on the European Circuit with his horse All In. The only reason he's even in need of a horse is that All In sustained an injury at the Rolex Grand Prix in Aachen, and Campbell needs a new horse to compete. All we ask is that you give him a chance."

Lionel paused for a moment. If this were anyone but Randall, he would be certain to ask just how All In had gotten hurt, and at a competition no less. That didn't bode well for the supposed talents of this 'special' rider. But then, he had known Randall for some time and trusted him. He didn't for a moment believe Randall would sponsor someone reckless enough to harm his horse, so Lionel relaxed.

"All right. If you really think he's the right person, bring him over as soon as possible. If we're going to get performances of the quality necessary to qualify for the Olympic Games, the pair will have to have as much time as possible together, both training and showing. You know as well as I do that time under saddle is the only way to establish the connection they need to compete at the highest levels."

"Thank you, Lionel. You won't regret this. I'll do everything I can to get the man over to your place tomorrow." "All right then, tomorrow it is. We'll see you then." Lionel ended the call, then turned toward Rachel, knowing she had been hanging on every word of his side of the conversation.

Rachel couldn't hide her impatience. "Well? What did he say?"

"He said he has an up-and-coming rider from Scotland that is truly special and that everyone is raving about. His name is Montgomery Campbell."

Rachel's brow wrinkled as she searched her memory for any information she might have heard about this potential rider for Beau. "I think I've heard of him. Although if memory serves, Monty, as he is more commonly known, has a reputation as an arrogant arse in addition to his talent as a rider."

Lionel groaned. "That's the last thing we need right now. Beau is too sensitive to let some arsehole who can ride better than most but thinks he's God's gift to the equestrian world climb aboard in the hopes he can control him. This could be a disaster."

Rachel grinned mischievously. "Actually, I'd like to see what happens when we put the two of them together."

Lionel looked at her as if she were crazy, then after thinking a bit, started to grin as well. "You're right. If this guy is as good as they say he is, Beau will perform spectacularly. If he isn't, Beau will have him on his arse in less than thirty seconds. Either way, it will certainly be entertaining."

Rachel winked at him. "My thoughts exactly."

The pair walked companionably down the barn aisle, Rachel occasionally stopping to speak with a barn worker to make sure everything was running smoothly. While Rachel was occupied, Lionel took a mental step back and marveled at the incredible transformation that Second Chance Farm had gone through since his disastrous mistake two years ago at the Olympic Trials.

The impact on his and his partner Nigel's lives had been instantaneous. Their once-thriving business had lost credibility in the British equestrian community overnight, and no one had suffered more than Nigel. His already- defective heart had ultimately proven too weak for him to continue training as a result of the additional stress caused by their precarious financial situation, and although he had been put on the list for a donor heart, a match couldn't be found in time. When Nigel passed away, Lionel was devastated at the loss.

Initially, in his despair over the loss of his livelihood and the love of his life, Lionel blamed Michael Stafford, and had taken steps to ruin Michael's life. He had been working diligently toward that goal when an abused horse named Rocky touched his heart and transformed Lionel's bitterness to self-reflection, then forgiveness. He experienced a profound reversal in a singular gesture of trust from a horse that had known nothing but neglect and vowed to work even harder to overcome the momentary lapse that had so publicly tarnished his reputation.

When he had confessed his sins to Michael, he fully expected him to reject him and never speak to him again. Instead, Michael had generously offered funds to assist Lionel in keeping Second Chance Farm in business.

If that weren't enough, Michael's brother Ian and Ian's wife Megan had taken things one step further and loaned him a substantial amount of money taken from their racehorse Seabiscuit II's winnings, and they had established a charitable foundation specifically to support Lionel's work with ex-race horses and other horses that had suffered abuse at the hands of cruel or negligent owners. Lionel vowed to do everything in his power to be worthy of their investment. Ian and Megan had not only sacrificed a substantial part of their wealth, but they had also put their reputations on the line for him.

Although Ian and Megan assured him that they could afford the expense, Lionel knew they were spending a substantial amount of money for security in the wake of the conviction of the notorious mob boss Seamus O'Reilly. Their lives were constantly in danger because O'Reilly was seeking revenge against Ian for the death of O'Reilly's son, Ryan. It was a guarantee that O'Reilly wouldn't forgive the killing, even though Ryan was killed because he had kidnapped Megan and was preparing to shoot Ian at point blank range when a member of Ian's security team killed him.

In the days, weeks, and months after receiving the Staffords' contributions, Lionel used the funds provided to scour the United Kingdom to find horses that needed not only re-training but rehabilitation. To Lionel's shock, there were almost too many to count.

He took on the horses he thought most amenable to rehabilitation and patiently worked with them to help them rediscover the trust that had been lost somewhere along the way. As he walked down the barn aisle taking in the many horses in various stages of training housed there, his heart swelled. Without the extra funding the Staffords had supplied, he would never have been able to care for or support all those horses, nor would he have been able to keep Rachel on as farm manager.

Lionel stopped in front of a stall occupied by one of his favorite horses on the farm, a huge, eighteen hand draft horse mare named Molly, and was greeted by a warm, deep- throated nicker. A big, scarred face lowered to meet Lionel and nudged him gently in the chest.

"How are you today, sweetheart?" Lionel gently stroked the face of the disfigured but still beautiful mare that he had rescued in the early days of his disgrace, when he took on practically every horse offered to him. Molly was a Belgian Draft horse that was no longer needed by her owner, a poor but stubborn farmer who refused to acknowledge he couldn't afford to keep all his livestock and have them stay healthy.

Lionel found Molly after a neighboring farmer contacted him. He found Molly emaciated and covered in mud, barely subsisting on the sparse grass in a small, mostly mud field. Her enclosure was surrounded by barbed wire, and on the day he arrived at the farm, she had somehow gotten her head entangled in the wire and cut herself badly.

Her owner hadn't the money to treat her, and her wounds would have easily festered without proper care. Using the funds the Staffords provided, Lionel purchased Molly on the spot from the farmer, and immediately called a vet for treatment. It didn't take long for Molly's golden chestnut coat and flaxen mane and tail to begin to glow as her overall health improved.

Her attitude benefitted somewhat as well. Even so, it seemed Lionel was the only person Molly would trust implicitly. She had mellowed a bit in the ensuing months, but she still saved her best behavior for Lionel. The mare seemed to know that Lionel had been her savior, and whenever Lionel visited the barn, Molly would raise a fuss if he didn't stop to see her.

After spending a few minutes loving on Molly, Lionel reconnected with Rachel, who had appeared at his side, reminding him that they had work to do. As they turned from Molly to proceed down the aisle, Lionel glanced quickly at the empty stall adjacent to Molly's that had the brass nameplate "Accolade" on the door.

A wave of sadness briefly overcame Lionel as he contemplated what might have been. As a result of Lionel's banishment, Accolade had to be sold and was now competing quite successfully for an experienced amateur rider. Although he was receiving some notoriety, Accolade never achieved the international status that Lionel had hoped he would. Lionel felt a burden of responsibility for that. After Accolade's sale, Lionel made certain that he would never experience neglect again. A condition of the sale that Lionel had insisted on was that once the rider was finished competing Accolade, he would be returned to Second Chance Farm for a peaceful and well- deserved retirement.

The pair continued down the aisle and stopped in front of the stall sporting a brass name plate with 'Gideon's Rainbow' engraved on it. A large, handsome bay horse with a black mane and tail and a white blaze that ran from his forehead to his muzzle stuck his head out.

The gelding Rachel had affectionately christened Beau nickered at them softly and nodded at them in greeting. With a gentle smile, Rachel began to absently stroke the gelding's forehead. She looked over at Lionel.

"You know, Lionel, I've also heard that Monty is very attractive, and definitely prefers men." She nudged Lionel gently with her shoulder. "It's been a while since you allowed that part of yourself to surface. You never know what could happen. You might even feel a spark."

Lionel inwardly cringed but couldn't blame Rachel for pushing. She had been working for Lionel and Nigel, managing their operation with grace and efficiency, since they opened Second Chance Farm seven years ago.

The two had met when Nigel, on one of his regular trips to the track, had witnessed Lionel being harassed and bullied by a group of racetrack toughs. He had seen Lionel before and knew of his reputation as an intuitive groom sought out by several trainers for his incredible ability to read horses. Nigel offered him a position away from the racetrack working with him. Lionel had gratefully agreed.

While living and working alongside Nigel, it didn't take long for Lionel to become attracted to the quiet, gentle man who had rescued him. Nigel, however, was patient and waited until Lionel got up the courage to approach him to begin a deeper, more physical and romantic relationship. After that, both their love and their business thrived.

With Lionel's help and support, Nigel took the further step of incorporating the enterprise, and the business attracted even more attention and clients. As their business grew, it became necessary to hire someone to help them manage the work required to keep the horses happy and the farm running smoothly, and Rachel came to them highly recommended. Although she was quite young, having just turned twenty- one, Rachel demonstrated a competence and common-sense approach to managing the horses in her care that made both Lionel and Nigel glad they had found her.

He smiled when he remembered Rachel's first few weeks at the farm and the exact moment when he realized that she had developed a crush on him. Although Nigel had teased Lionel about Rachel's infatuation, Lionel had struggled to find a way to let her know he wasn't attracted to her in that way.

He was saved from having to take that uncomfortable step when about a month into her employment she inadvertently walked into the farm's main tack room and found Nigel and Lionel in a passionate embrace, and, with a mumbled apology and quite a bit of blushing, quickly exited the room. He grinned to himself at the remembrance. He didn't know who was more embarrassed at the time— Rachel or the two men.

To this day, Lionel couldn't understand what had drawn Rachel or Nigel to him. Lionel saw himself as tall and skinny, with unruly and unremarkable light blond hair and common, blue eyes. Although Nigel had assured him he was classically handsome, Lionel wasn't quite sure he agreed with that assessment. Now, at the ripe old age of thirty-five, he was certainly not someone he would consider swoon worthy. There was no way he could be attractive to a young, flamboyant personality that Monty Campbell was reputed to be.

Lionel snorted. "A relationship is the last thing I need right now, Rachel. Besides, what would a young, energetic stud like Campbell see in a stodgy old fag like me?"

Rachel frowned and smacked Lionel on the arm. "Lionel, stop putting yourself down. From what I've read, Monty is twenty-five, which is only ten years younger than you. You are not stodgy, and you're not old. What you are is lonely and isolated. Since Nigel died, you've taken yourself out of the social world and dedicated yourself only to your work. Lionel, you owe it to yourself and to Nigel's memory to live. Nigel would not have wanted you to shut yourself away and life half a life. He would have wanted you to be happy."

Lionel knew Rachel only meant to help, but as far as he was concerned, his love life was not open for discussion. He recognized the concerned expression on Rachel's face and had seen it on more than one occasion recently. This would have to be handled delicately. He took Rachel gently by both shoulders and looked her squarely in the eyes. "Rachel, I consider you one of my closest friends, and I love you dearly, but please let me decide how to live my life."

Rachel winced. "I'm sorry, Lionel. It's just that I hate to see you living half a life. I remember how happy you and Nigel were, but he's gone now. It's time for you to move on."

He sighed, "I wish moving on and being happy was as easy as you make it sound." He dropped his hands from Rachel's shoulders and looked away. If only there were someone he could love as much as he had loved Nigel. The closeness the two of them had shared would be difficult, if not impossible to find again. His mind drifted back to a day when he and Nigel had spent a long, exhausting afternoon working with a very difficult horse.

The stallion had been abused to the point of serious injury by his owners, and as a result of the abuse, to prevent anyone from every getting close enough to hurt him again, he constantly threatened to kill anyone that came within his reach. They had tried everything they could think of to reach the trusting spirit that had once existed in this animal, until finally they found a key to gaining his trust.

After putting their heads together, both Lionel and Nigel decided that they would have to show the horse that they trusted him before he would ever take a step toward trusting them. They used a round pen and herded the horse in first to allow him to acclimate, then both men entered the pen unencumbered by tools, ropes, or other modes of control and stood a few meters apart facing away from him.

At first, the horse made threatening moves toward them and snorted his aggression. The men stayed completely still, not reacting either aggressively or submissively. As they had hoped, it wasn't long for the stallion they knew to be highly intelligent became curious, and cautiously approached each man. In turn, he would sniff them, and eventually even nudged them with his nose to see what their reaction would be. When the men didn't react at all, the stallion seemed to shed his protective shields and began to ignore their presence, essentially accepting them as they were.

When their patience was finally rewarded with a visible surrender from the once dangerously fearful horse, they had embraced each other in triumph, tears streaming from their faces. He had never felt closer to Nigel nor loved him more in that moment. He was suddenly hit with a tremendous feeling of emptiness. *God, I miss him.*

Overcome with grief at the memory, he forced himself back to the present and looked earnestly at Rachel, his voice choked with unshed tears. "Nigel was my whole life, Rachel. He and I had a connection that surpassed the labels of 'partner' or 'lover.' Without him, I feel as though I'm half a man."

Rachel reached out to Lionel, and he could tell that she regretted that her well-intended efforts to match-make had only succeeded in re-awakening Lionel's grief. She placed her hand gently on his shoulder.

"I'm so sorry, Lionel. I didn't mean to bring back painful memories."

Lionel loved Rachel too much to allow her to take the blame for his temporary lapse into grief, and struggled to control his emotions, rubbed the tears from his eyes, and when he had regained his composure, said, "It's all right, sweetheart. It just reinforces for me that it will take someone very special to fill that tremendous void. From what you've told me, Monty Campbell is not going to be that person."

Rachel moved closer to Lionel and slipped slowly into a hug as Lionel wrapped his arms gently around her. She smiled up at him and said, "You know, Lionel, you're probably right."

Chapter 2

"Yes, Ma. I've seen him, and he's going to be all right." Monty Campbell paced up and down in the waiting area, where he was finally allowed to use his cell phone to call his nearly frantic mother.

Since Monty was now living in Edinburgh, his was the first number the EMT's called after they found his younger brother, Gavin, in an abandoned warehouse in Edinburgh suffering from a heroin overdose. They immediately treated him with Naloxone and rushed him to the Royal Edinburgh hospital.

"Do you know who called the ambulance, Monty?" his mother asked. "Whoever it was, we owe them a tremendous debt of gratitude. They most likely saved his life."

"I don't know who called the ambulance, Ma, but it was probably whoever was there with him shooting up." Thank God they had the presence of mind to call someone, or his mother was right—Gavin would be dead.

"How soon can he come home from the hospital?"

"The doctors want to keep him for a few hours for observation, then they will release him. Just get here as quickly as you can. I'm not sure he would go home if you weren't here to take him. I'd stay, but I must go to Hickstead tomorrow to look at a jumper prospect. The British national equestrian organization thinks this horse is hugely talented and will be able to get me to the World Cup and even to the Olympics."

"Oh my God, Monty! The Olympics! Truly?"

"Yes, Ma, the Olympics. And I have you and Dad to thank for that. Without your support from the time you bought me my first pony and hauled me all over the country to shows and lessons, to the tremendous sacrifice you made to put a second mortgage on the house to buy me All In, I'm so very grateful. But now that All In is out of commission, I need a new mount. This is an appointment I can't afford to miss. It's that important."

Not that Monty didn't love his brother, but this wasn't the first time Gavin had gotten himself in trouble, nor was it his first drug overdose. Now that he was in the hospital and under a doctor's care, Gavin was in the best possible place.

"All right, sweetheart. Your father and I will be there as soon as possible. Probably within the hour."

"OK, Ma. I'll see you soon." He hung up and walked back to Gavin's room to keep watch until his mother arrived. Gavin was just as he'd left him, hooked up to IV's and on a heart monitor to ensure there weren't any complications following his treatment with Naloxone.

Although when he first arrived at the hospital, Gavin had been awake and responsive, the doctors told Monty that he had drifted into an exhausted sleep not long after they placed him in the bed.

Monty's heart clenched at the sight of his twenty-one- year-old brother lying pale, gaunt and helpless in his hospital bed. His once glorious head of auburn hair now matted and dirty, and the clothing he was wearing at the time the EMT's found him was fit only for the dust bin. It seemed like only yesterday that the two of them had been playing football together in the family's backyard, laughing and roughhousing as if they didn't have a care in the world.

Monty blamed himself for Gavin's current state. After all, this all started soon after Monty moved out of the family home to make a name for himself in the world of international show jumping. Not long after Monty left, his parents called to inform him that Gavin had changed.

First, he had started running with a dodgy crowd, who, Monty later learned, encouraged Gavin to experiment with prescription opioid drugs first, then, when those no longer satisfied his craving for the ultimate high, he escalated to heroin.

Their parents had tried everything they could think of to get Gavin to admit he was addicted and seek treatment, but initially he was having too much fun, and didn't understand how much his body was beginning to crave the drug. It didn't take long, however, once he started shooting up heroin, that the craving for the drug, and the hell his body and mind went through when he didn't get it right away, drove him out of the family home and into the streets.

Monty shuddered to think of what his little brother might have had to do to earn the money he needed to buy those necessary hits. As he stared at Gavin lying helpless in the hospital bed, he looked like he hadn't eaten in days. It had been months since their parents had heard from him, and even then, he had only been in contact to ask for money. As much as his parents loved Gavin, they refused to support his heroin habit. Instead, they had offered to take him to rehab, but Gavin was having none of it and stalked out. They hadn't seen him since.

As if sensing his brother's presence, Gavin slowly opened his eyes, immediately wincing at the bright sunlight entering the room through his window, not to mention the florescent hospital lights, and probably also at the pain he was experiencing now that the numbness of the drugs' effects was wearing off.

When Gavin's gaze fell on Monty, he immediately frowned. "If it isn't the big star of the equestrian world. What are you doing here? Don't you have some competition to be at?" His voice sounded hoarse, so Monty quickly grabbed a glass of water and offered it to him. Gavin grudgingly took a couple of sips through the straw then relaxed back to his bed and turned away from Monty to stare blankly out the hospital room window.

Monty wasn't necessarily surprised by Gavin's immediate rejection, but a part of him was hurt by it all the same.

"I'm here to make sure you're OK until Ma and Dad get here to take over."

"Tell them not to bother. They made it crystal clear the last time I saw them that they wanted nothing to do with me."

Gavin's surly attitude was the last straw as far as Monty was concerned. "That's only because you came to them asking for money for more drugs. Can you blame them for refusing? They love you and hate to see you suffer, but the last thing you need is more of the poison that landed you here. You need to go to rehab or the next time you OD, it may be your last."

Seeing that Gavin had effectively tuned him out, Monty turned to leave the room, then hesitated. He knew it was imperative that he and his family used this opportunity to convince Gavin he had to get clean. It was true that they hadn't seen him in months. It was only the fact that he still carried a wallet with his driver's license in it that his family even knew he was here.

Just then, Monty heard his mother's voice down the hall. It wasn't long before she and their father appeared. They looked at Monty, their concern for their youngest son blatantly apparent.

"How is he?" his father asked.

"Ask him yourself. He woke up just a few minutes ago," Monty replied.

At that news, both parents tentatively entered Gavin's room, unsure of their reception.

It appeared that Gavin wasn't interested in talking, and his parents looked at Monty as if asking for his help in overcoming Gavin's rejection. He shrugged, helpless to figure out the brother that had now become a stranger.

Gavin started coughing and both parents reached for the water to try to do something to help, their attention focused back on the son they desperately wanted to help. Monty again felt the pain of responsibility. At the same time, he knew that right now there was nothing he could do to help Gavin. It was up to his brother to make the decision and take steps to wean himself off the heroin.

Monty punched the doorframe in frustration. He knew that Gavin was an adult and was responsible for the consequences of his own actions, but Monty had always been the older brother. The one responsible for his brother's wellbeing. He felt so helpless. There had to be something he could do. He had been winning some of the more prestigious competitions lately and racked up some impressive purses.

Maybe he could convince Gavin to go to a private rehab center rather than be put on a waiting list for the NHS rehab treatment centers. Too bad Monty's brilliant horse, All In, had been injured in a freak accident and he had to find a new horse. Hopefully, this horse Gideon's Rainbow would be the answer to his prayers.

Chapter 3

Lionel watched as a late-model black Range Rover traveled up the farm drive and stopped in the nearby parking area. As soon as the vehicle engine was shut off, two men exited the vehicle. He recognized the man exiting the driver's side of the vehicle as Randall Bridges. Randall had always been a bit cagey when it came to admitting his age, but Lionel guessed that Randall was in his early sixties.

What Lionel knew for a certainty was that Randall always presented a distinguished appearance with his wavy salt and pepper hair perfectly styled. Today he was wearing a tweed jacket, crew neck sweater, and designer jeans with western boots, which was his usual uniform.

Lionel had a fondness for Randall because he was the first member of the British equestrian establishment that was willing to forgive Lionel's transgression and give him another chance. For that, Lionel would always be in Randall's debt.

The second man drew Lionel's interest from the moment he exited the car. He was a couple of inches over six feet tall, with thick, wavy auburn hair that seemed to defy any attempts at taming. He was clearly young, which confirmed Rachel's recollection that he was about twenty-five, and had an air of confidence bordering on arrogance Lionel rarely saw in someone that young. He was dressed more casually than Randall, wearing a polo shirt and breeches. Lionel noted with approval that he was already wearing his riding boots, meaning he was eager to climb aboard Beau and give him a try.

So, this is Monty Campbell. At that moment, Randall turned to Monty and said something that drew his attention. Lionel took advantage of the distraction Randall provided to look the young Scot over further. Lionel had to admit that he was incredibly handsome, tall, and fit, without being overly muscular. *If only I were ten years younger.* Lionel caught himself short. Where did that thought come from? Disconcerted by the direction of his wayward thoughts. Lionel mentally shook himself and fixed a smile on his face and stepped forward to greet the two men.

"Gentlemen," he said as he shook hands with each of them in turn. "Welcome to Second Chance Farm." He looked directly at Monty. "Mr. Campbell, I'm Lionel Hayes. It's a pleasure to meet you. Randall has been singing your praises, and I must confess I'm looking forward to seeing what you can do with Gideon's Rainbow." Before the man could respond, Lionel turned and started to lead the two men to the barn. "My farm manager, Rachel, is in the barn tacking up Beau as we speak. He should be ready for you in a few minutes."

"I'm really looking forward to seeing Gideon's Rainbow in action," Randall effused. "I've heard such great things about him."

"He is special," Lionel assured him. "You won't be disappointed."

Monty took the opportunity to interject. "If you don't mind, Lionel, I think I'll withhold judgment until I have to chance to try him myself. It wouldn't be the first time an owner has puffed up a horse's abilities to make a sale." He then turned to Randall and said in a low voice, although not low enough that Lionel wasn't able to hear him, "I hope you aren't wasting my time here, Randall. I don't have much time to find a replacement for All In, and this farm doesn't impress me as the kind of place that would produce a world class jumper."

Lionel's temper flared. It took everything he had not to give this young man the set down he deserved. It appeared Rachel was right. This man was too arrogant by half. Not someone he would ever consider a romantic partner. Now he was really looking forward to Beau's reaction to the man. This could be very interesting. Pointedly ignoring Monty's rude comment, he turned to an embarrassed Randall and asked after his family.

AS LIONEL AND RANDALL conversed, Monty took the opportunity to examine Lionel more closely. He had been drawn to the tall, handsome blond man standing near the barn entrance from the time he and Randall had started up the drive. Somehow, he hadn't expected Lionel Hayes to be so incredibly attractive.

When Lionel had approached them and smiled his welcome, Monty's heart had skipped a beat. *Be still my heart. How am I going to resist that smile?* Monty cursed to himself as his undisciplined cock had reacted to Lionel's appearance. If this was how his body was going to react when he was seeing Lionel for the first time, how was he going to keep himself in check after they got to know each other better? If this tryout worked as he hoped, this was going to be a difficult season, especially if Lionel were kept on as an assistant trainer for Monty and Beau as they competed. Randall had confirmed that would surely be the case.

Monty frowned as he remembered that when he had allowed himself to get too close to his trainer in the past, it hadn't worked out very well. In fact, the one time he had previously fallen for his trainer, who had also been a gorgeous older man, he had been hurt badly. Never again.

His purposely rude comment to Randall served to ensure Lionel would believe the rumors and keep his distance from Monty. He had learned early on that older men eager for a liaison with a handsome young man wouldn't hesitate to approach him. It wasn't until he cultivated a reputation as an arrogant, self-centered arse that men gave him the distance he preferred.

"Is something wrong?" Lionel, it appeared, had noticed his frown.

"No, nothing at all. I think I must have eaten something that disagreed with me for lunch. I'm fine."

"If you'd like to postpone, we can," Lionel offered, concern evident in his expression.

"I told you, it's nothing." Monty resumed his cool manner.

Lionel hesitated, as if sensing there was more to Monty's pained expression than a bad meal, but ultimately seemed satisfied with his response, and the group continued to the stable.

Monty resolved to keep his focus on the upcoming ride and succeeded in pushing his memories aside. Back in the present, however, Monty watched Lionel walking with Randall in front of him, and couldn't help admiring his well- shaped buttocks, encased in tight-fitting riding breeches. *He's off-limits, remember?* Monty took a deep breath and tried to focus on his plan for riding Gideon's Rainbow. He still found his thoughts drifting toward the man walking in front of him. *Bloody hell!*

Not that it mattered, he mused. Lionel was famously still grieving over his deceased lover, and from all accounts had not dated or even been seen in public with another man since Nigel Crawford's death. Monty was surprised at the depth of the disappointment he felt at that fact.

As they entered the barn, Monty saw a bay horse just under seventeen hands tall, with black mane and tail and a white blaze standing quietly in cross ties while a young woman put the finishing touches on his tack. She was just tightening the horse's girth, when the gelding heard them approach and turned to examine them.

Monty immediately noticed the intelligence reflected in the horse's gaze, and the moment their gazes locked, he could swear that the horse communicated silently to him that he was happy to see him and ready to perform for him. In that split second, Monty knew with a certainty that shocked him that this horse was meant for him.

His silent communication with the horse was interrupted when the young woman tacking him up reached out her hand in greeting. "Hello. I'm Rachel Adams—Lionel's barn manager and all-around caretaker."

"Monty Campbell," Monty replied, absently taking her hand in his for a brief shake. He uttered a perfunctory "A pleasure to meet you," but had not once taken his attention off the horse in front of him. "And this must be Gideon's Rainbow."

"It is." Rachel's smile was strained. She had not failed to notice that Monty had practically ignored her in favor of the horse he was there to ride. "We like to call him Beau for short." She shot a mischievous grin at Lionel. "We're pretty informal around here."

Lionel cleared his throat, appearing somewhat uncomfortable for a few seconds, he frowned at Rachel for a fraction of a second, then addressed Monty. "What Rachel means is that we don't stand on formality here, so please don't hesitate to let us know if there's anything you need."

Monty thought for a moment, then replied, "There's really nothing more I need right now. Let's get to it. Is it all right if I lead Beau out and warm him up a bit before we get started?"

"Certainly," Lionel said. "Our dressage arena is open and ready for you. There's a mounting block out there, and I have a crop if you think you might need one. The jumping course is in the next arena, and you can walk him over there under saddle if you like. He's used to it."

"Thanks," Monty replied. "About the crop, let me see how he goes, and I'll let you know if I need it."

As he took his riding gloves out of his back pocket, Monty studied the big gelding closely. Beau seemed calm, almost too calm considering the amount of tension Monty himself felt at being here. He knew he was being tested as much as the horse.

From what he had already heard, it seemed that nearly everyone that saw Gideon's Rainbow jump were completely overcome by his amazing talent. He glanced back at Lionel. Was it possible Hayes was back to his doping habits again? Was that why this horse was performing so spectacularly? He mentally shook himself. Randall and the British Equestrian authorities would never have recommended him if there was even a hint of illegality. He dismissed his concerns and turned to focus all his attention on the horse.

From what Randall had told him on the way to the farm, Lionel hadn't had an inkling of Beau's talent for jumping until several months into his training. Normally, for his business to be successful, Lionel was only required to train his horses to the point where another, most likely amateur, rider would be able to take over.

When Lionel trained Beau, as he did with most of his off-the-track horses, he started with dressage, which was his area of expertise. Most horses welcomed the steadiness and predictability of the twenty-meter circles, diagonals, and serpentines of training level dressage. Beau, however, gave him nothing but trouble. Randall had chuckled when he related that Lionel learned quickly that Beau was bored with the basics of dressage.

As Randall had continued explaining Beau's background it was clear that he was impressed with Lionel's patience and creativity in his approach to Beau. He went on to explain that to engage the gelding's active mind, Lionel started working Beau over ground poles, or *cavalletti*. It didn't take long before Lionel also set a short jump at the end of a series of *cavalletti*, and Beau was all in. From there, the jumps just kept getting bigger and more challenging, and Beau had yet to meet a jump he would refuse.

It wasn't long before rumors began circulating that Lionel had a horse that was spectacular over jumps. At that point, the only block that hadn't been checked to make Beau a competitive show jumper was show experience. After Beau won several rated competitions in spectacular fashion, Lionel was soon approached by several trainers who thought that the horse would be perfect for their more ambitious students.

At this point in the narrative, Randall had advised Monty to proceed with caution. It seemed that when amateur riders attempted to ride Beau over jumps, he became resistant and misbehaved. In some cases, he would even buck off the rider. It seemed that Beau could instantly sense the level of expertise of the rider and would only perform for someone whom he could trust to handle him competently. If he didn't get that sense from the very beginning, the rider was destined for the ground.

With that last caveat in mind, Monty ascended the mounting block and calmly mounted Beau. After quickly settling himself in the saddle and taking his stirrups, he spoke softly to the horse, earning the gelding's undivided attention. "Give me a break, will you, old man?" Monty whispered. "If you do this for me, I promise I'll let you show off to your heart's content."

When Beau snorted in response, Monty took that as an agreement, and urged the gelding forward into a working walk, then, when he was satisfied the horse was moving without tension, he moved into a smooth, working trot. While in trot, Monty rode some basic flat work patterns to continue to warm them both up. All the while, he watched the gelding's ears flip back and forth as if trying to determine how good a rider he had on his back. When Monty believed they were both sufficiently warmed up, he took a deep breath and asked Beau for some collection at the trot.

After the slightest bit of hesitation, Beau softened his back and his jaw and engaged his powerful hindquarters to surge forward. The effect for Monty was akin to floating. He tried unsuccessfully to suppress the giddy grin that spread across his face. *My God, this horse is fantastic!* Almost at the same time, Monty felt Beau breathe deeply and relax throughout his body. It appeared Monty had proven himself worthy.

Now that he felt more comfortable with the horse, Monty walked him over to the jump arena, and urged him into a smooth, rocking canter. After a turn around the perimeter of the arena, he set Beau at some jumps that had been set up in the center of the arena. The first was a 1.6-meter vertical jump made up of four horizontal poles painted in brilliant blue and white stripes. Beau's ears pricked forward, and he took the jump with ease. After similar results with an international class oxer, a wall, and a triple combination, Monty was ecstatic. He wanted this horse.

Chapter 4

Lionel watched Monty's approach to Beau with interest as the horse and rider slowly but surely began to learn each other. He saw the gelding respond to the young Scot as if the man had ridden and trained the horse for years. Lionel felt a pang of jealousy that someone could so easily master his complicated jumper.

He also felt something he thought he would never feel again: desire for the handsome young man, quickly followed by guilt. How could he possibly be attracted to another man so soon after Nigel's death? Granted, it had been over a year since Nigel's passing, but surely he owed him a period of mourning. Just then, Rachel's words from yesterday came back to him: *Nigel would not have wanted you to shut yourself away and life half a life. He would have wanted you to be happy.*

Rachel wasn't wrong. When they both realized that Nigel's life was growing short, Nigel had, on several occasions, made Lionel promise not to spend the rest of his life alone. At the time, the concept of life without Nigel had been impossible, but he had made the promise to make Nigel happy. Today, he had, for the first time since Nigel's passing, felt desire for another man. It's too bad this man was nothing like Nigel, and his attitude didn't attract Lionel in the least.

At that moment, Rachel who had been standing beside him since they had yielded Beau to Monty, whispered in Lionel's ear, "Look at that. They look like they've known each other for years, not minutes."

"You're right," he acknowledged, firmly back in the present. "From what you told me about Monty's reputation, I didn't expect him to be sensitive enough to understand Beau, much less ride him with such an intuitive feel. But he does it easily without being overly aggressive. I have to admit I'm impressed."

Randall overheard Lionel's last statement and grinned with satisfaction. "Does that mean we have a chance to make a match?"

Lionel glanced at Rachel, then smiled at Randall. "I think we should be able to work something out. Once Monty is finished, let's go inside and discuss the details over tea."

Lionel didn't notice that Randall's expression turned from pleased to strained at the mention of the details of Beau's transfer.

After Monty returned Beau to Lionel, his face sported an ecstatic smile. He reached out to shake Lionel's hand. "Thank you so much for allowing me the chance to try Beau out. He's fantastic, and I believe, if you allow me to have him, the two of us together will do great things for Britain." Lionel struggled to bring his focus to what Monty was saying. He was desperately fighting to maintain some sense of gravitas in the face of the fierce sense of attraction he felt for Monty in that moment.

That feeling was soon eclipsed by a jolt of awareness he felt when Monty shook his hand. He studied Monty's face to see if he had a similar reaction but saw no sign that the young man got a similar jolt. *It figures. The first man to stir my senses since Nigel, and he doesn't feel a jot of attraction to me. Just as well, he's still arrogant and conceited. Not my type at all.*

The lack of reaction from Monty acted as a cold reminder to Lionel that these men were here purely for business. He instantly shifted his focus to the transaction at hand. "I was just telling Randall that I don't see any reason why we can't come to an agreement. I would be lying if I said you looked anything but spectacular on Beau. I could tell he was attuned to you almost from the beginning."

"Actually," Monty countered, "he was feeling me out at first, but because Randall had prepared me for a bit of a test from Beau, I stayed steady and didn't allow him to rattle me. It didn't take long before he realized I could ride him and not allow him to overpower or outmaneuver me. After that, we got along just fine."

Even as he noted the implied conceit in that statement, Lionel noticed that Monty was surreptitiously studying him, and a flash of desire crossed the young Scot's features before he could mask it. Lionel's pulse quickened when he realized Monty might be interested in him, then he hastily brought himself back under control. Monty had already schooled his features to mask his desire, and Lionel resolved that even though this inconvenient attraction was potentially mutual, he had to keep his relationship with Monty on a purely professional basis.

"I believe you when you say that the two of you will do great things for Britain. After watching you together, I'm certain of it." He motioned to both men to follow and turned toward the house. Let's go sit down and work this sale out." Monty grinned his approval. "You won't be sorry, Lionel. I guarantee it."

Oh, for heaven's sake. Lionel suppressed a sarcastic smile and started walking toward his home, expecting Randall and Monty to follow. Randall hesitated, and Lionel looked back at his friend with some concern.

"Is there something wrong?"

"Actually, Lionel, I fear you have a mistaken impression of how this transaction is going to go forward."

Lionel stiffened as if preparing for a blow. "What do you mean? I expected that this would be a simple sale of a horse to the British Equestrian Team, or to a sponsor who has stepped forward to purchase the horse for Monty to ride. Am I mistaken?"

"Unfortunately, there are members of the national body that have long memories and are hesitant to purchase a horse from a man who has been proven capable of drugging a competition horse."

Lionel grimaced. "Don't tell me, let me guess. It's Rex Masterson isn't it? He was the most strident voice at the time I was banned and has never forgotten my single moment of weakness." Lionel started pacing in agitation. "Tell me, will I ever be accepted by the authorities? What do I have to do? Isn't two years without as much as a traffic violation enough time to prove my commitment to change?"

Randall had the grace to look ashamed. "I'm sorry, Lionel. What the Team has dictated is that we lease Gideon's Rainbow from you for the season, subject to random drug testing, and if he is successful and drug free for the season, at the end of the calendar year a purchase will be negotiated."

"And if something happens to him during the season, or if there's a hint of a scintilla of a banned substance in his blood?" Lionel asked, barely concealing his rage.

"In that case, the horse will be returned to you, and all dealings will cease immediately."

"Of course." Lionel couldn't keep the sarcasm out of his voice. "I should have guessed that would be the result." Lionel looked at Rachel, whose stricken expression reflected his own initial shock at the British Equestrian Team's blatant mistrust of him. Of course, he should have expected something like this. The British equestrian authorities were conservative in the extreme, and he had after all proven to be a one-time cheater.

"I assume I don't even get to accompany Beau and assist in his care while Monty is riding him?"

"On the contrary. The Team has agreed that you and one of your staff—I assume that will be Rachel—will accompany the horse and ensure he is taken care of and that Monty has the benefit of your advice. You have been Beau's sole trainer and have insights no other person would have. The team trusts you that much."

"Only because they have the random drug tests to keep me honest, Randall. Don't forget that. I am not convinced I have anyone's trust, except maybe yours."

"You do have my trust." Randall placed his hand on Lionel's shoulder and squeezed gently, "Let's go inside and have some tea. We need to work out a reasonable lease fee for Beau that will cover everything and ensure you're covered in case something happens to him due to Monty's negligence or other circumstances beyond your control."

Once inside, Randall handed Lionel a document that was several pages long. Lionel flipped through the document and groaned to himself. There was no way he could read and understand all the legal mumbo jumbo, and Randall acknowledged as much.

"The Team provided a draft document, but before you sign anything, please consult with a solicitor to make sure your interests are sufficiently covered."

Lionel smiled, but the expression didn't reach his eyes. "Don't worry, Randall, I will most certainly consult a legal advisor before I sign anything." He struggled to maintain his composure considering these new, very distressing developments, and finally succeeded. "Now, how about that tea?"

As Rachel poured tea for all of them, Lionel surreptitiously glanced a Monty to gauge his reaction to his conversation with Randall. From the look of absolute shock on his face, it was apparent that Monty had had no idea of the British Equestrian Team's intent that Beau be leased rather than purchased from Lionel. Lionel took some comfort from that. He admitted to himself that he would have been incredibly heartbroken if Monty had been a party to this plan.

Sometime later, as they watched the Range Rover pull out of the driveway, Rachel faced Lionel. "I'm so sorry, Lionel. The authorities are treating you abominably."

"I suppose I should have expected it." He sighed. "It's all right. I'll have our solicitor look at the proposal. She'll probably tweak a few things so they don't have all the advantages, and this will work out."

Rachel nodded. "You know, though, that once all the details are worked out Beau and Monty are going to clean up in competition."

Lionel thought back to the sight of Monty masterfully jumping Beau and he felt another jolt of desire. He forced himself to avoid

Rachel's eyes because he knew after their years of working closely together, Rachel would be able to read him like a book.

His fears were confirmed when Rachel looked at him with a spark of mischief in her eyes. "Am I crazy, or did I detect a bit of a spark between you and young Mr. Campbell?" Lionel surprised himself by blushing a bit at the question.

He struggled to maintain a serious demeanor, but when he looked at Rachel, he knew he wasn't going to prevaricate. Rachel was as good a friend as he could ever hope to have, and he wasn't about to keep anything this important a secret from her.

He sighed and failed to suppress a sheepish grin. "You may have, Rachel. I have to admit I felt something when we shook hands, and that feeling grew when I watched him ride Beau." He kicked at a pebble with the toe of his boot. "I don't know for certain whether he feels the same way, but I got the distinct feeling he was interested."

Rachel frowned. "It's too bad the man is such an arrogant arse. I can't see the two of you together at all."

Lionel grimaced. Maybe he shouldn't have said anything to Rachel after all. She was right, though. The man was clearly arrogant and self-centered. His disparaging remarks about Second Chance Farm were especially infuriating. At least it would make it easier to relegate his attraction to Monty as just a physical attraction to a handsome face and athletic body. Nothing more than superficial lust, easily conquered.

"You're right, darling," he said. "This way it makes it easy to keep our relationship on a strictly business footing. You saw how arrogant and conceited he was. Those traits don't attract me in the least. Not to mention the fact that we're several years apart in age. He could have any man he wanted, why would he choose me?" It was then that he realized there might be another, even more serious reason why Monty might not want to be associated with him.

"Remember, too, Rachel, that I have a rather spotty reputation in the equestrian world. If he aspires to international competition and a spot on the British Olympic Team, he would be wise to stay completely away from me. There's no telling what the press might do if they learn we have a relationship outside of the professional."

Rachel frowned. "Lionel, that was a long time ago, and in the eyes of most of the country's professionals, you've redeemed yourself many times over. Please don't let your past keep you from achieving the happiness you deserve."

Lionel nodded, but he was not convinced. "The public and the press love a scandal, and my redemption wouldn't get nearly the press that a rehash of my disgrace would. It only takes one salacious story to rekindle the entire mess. I wouldn't wish that on anyone, and especially not on someone I care for. If I pursued him, Monty could easily become one of those people."

Rachel hooked her arm through Lionel's. "I suppose you're right. But enough of this depressing conversation. Let's go tell Beau that he's about to be a superstar."

Lionel grinned; his troubles forgotten for just a few minutes. "Yes, let's."

The pair approached Beau's stall and the gelding poked his head over the stall door and nickered a welcome.

Lionel scratched the horse's nose. "You look supremely satisfied with yourself, boy. I think you know you've found the right rider that will take you as far as your talents will allow."

Beau nodded emphatically, as if he understood everything Lionel had said and agreed wholeheartedly with him.

Lionel and Rachel exchanged a look and laughed.

"I don't think we have anything to worry about with this one," Rachel said. "He's ready for the spotlight."

"He certainly is," Lionel agreed, but his enthusiasm was dampened by a sense of dread. There was a cloud hanging over him because of his past, and there was nothing he could do about it.

Chapter 5

Mickey Collins strode briskly behind the uniformed corrections officer, his steps echoed in the brightly lit, concrete-walled hallway in the heart of Wakefield Prison. Even he, who had begun his criminal career as a youth picking pockets on the mean streets of Dublin, escalating to robbery then murder as Seamus O'Reilly's right hand, shuddered at the level of depravity of the criminals housed in this prison.

Dubbed the "Monster Mansion," Wakefield housed some of the U.K.'s most dangerous criminals. Mickey was here to visit Seamus, who to this day, even though convicted and sentenced to life in prison for multiple murders, kidnappings, and other major crimes, remained his boss and the head of one of Ireland's most notorious crime families.

The two men stopped at a door, and the corrections officer unlocked it with a passkey. He opened the door into an expansive beige linoleum-floored room filled with several round Formica-topped tables. Each table was surrounded by four vinyl-covered chairs. At this moment, none of the tables in the room was occupied. *Curious, that.*

"Right this way, Mr. Collins," the man said. "Please take a seat. Mr. O'Reilly will be brought out to see you in a few minutes."

Mr. O'Reilly? It was then that Mickey realized what was going on, and why. He smiled to himself. It appeared the boss was very much the boss, even in this notorious prison. Somehow, the guards had been co-opted, and were doing whatever they could get away with to make Seamus' life easier while he spent the rest of his life in prison.

No doubt Seamus had promised the men some type of monetary compensation for their efforts. Of course, Mickey mused, the warden would be none the wiser, if the men knew what was good for them. Mickey sat back and waited for the boss to make his appearance.

It wasn't long before the door on the far side of the room opened, and Seamus entered, flanked by two burly guards. Mickey was a bit surprised to see that but for the bright- orange jumpsuit, Seamus looked as he always had before his arrest and conviction—arrogant, confident, and the master of all he surveyed. As soon as he saw Mickey, Seamus' face broke into a broad, toothy smile. He strode toward him, while the guards took positions on either side of the exit door.

Seamus enveloped Mickey in a heartfelt embrace. After releasing him, Seamus showed Mickey to a chair and took a seat opposite him. "Mickey, my boy," Seamus exclaimed, "How are you, lad? What brings you to my humble abode on this fine day?"

Mickey fought the urge to roll his eyes, lowered his voice and responded, "You know as well as I do that it was you that summoned me to visit, Seamus. What is it you need from me?"

Seamus looked around to make sure the guards weren't paying close attention, then winked at Mickey. "Rest easy, lad. I just wanted to find out how much progress you've made on the project I set out for you last month."

"Ah, yes, that." Mickey wiped a hand over his face and grimaced. "It's been more difficult than I expected to find anything I can use against the Stafford family directly. Michael and Jessica Stafford are clean as a whistle and have been spending most of their time in America. Ian and Megan Stafford are heavily guarded by a combination of local police and his friend's security firm. No easy pickings in either case."

"Bollocks!" Seamus slammed his fist on the table, immediately drawing the attention of the guards standing nearby. Mickey met their stares and shook his head slightly to indicate they shouldn't worry. Seamus and his temper were very familiar to him. "There must be something we can do. Ian Stafford killed my son Ryan and I want him or someone he holds dear to pay. Look into their friends and personal connections. Isn't there anyone in the Stafford's circle of friends that's vulnerable to attack?"

Mickey stared at the table, wracking his brain to see if he could think of someone within the Stafford family's acquaintance that might have a vulnerability they could use. He thought about individuals he knew were close to the Stafford family. One name quickly rose to the surface.

"I've got it!" he exclaimed. "Do you remember a couple of years ago the bloke who was caught drugging his horse, and was disqualified from competing in the Olympic Games?"

"Vaguely," Seamus replied, not quite understanding why Mickey was so enthused.

"If my memory serves, that man was Lionel Hayes, who also happens to be Michael Stafford's best friend."

"So what if he is?" Seamus retorted. "That happened long ago. The public has long forgotten about that."

Mickey swallowed his frustration, knowing that Seamus would not tolerate any hint of disrespect. *He was never much of a creative thinker.* "Think about it, boss. The latest news is that Hayes is back in the British equestrian establishment's good graces and has a horse that is again capable of qualifying for the Olympics. This time it's a jumper. Not only that, both Michael and Ian Stafford have invested heavily in Hayes' rehabilitation farm, and Ian and Megan Stafford have established a charity in his name. They are counting on his being able to sell this star horse to the British Equestrian Team to recoup their investment.

"If we can find someone to frame Hayes and make it look like he's back to his old ways of doping just when he's finally managed to rehabilitate his reputation, he'll be banned from equestrian circles for life, no one will want to touch the horse, and the Staffords will lose their investment.

The Staffords' reputations will be ruined as well. Michael and Jessica Stafford's good standing will be tainted by their close association with Hayes, and Ian and Megan Stafford will be lucky if they stay in good stead with the Racing Commission once they're found to be financially supporting a known doper. Most certainly their charity will be ignobly shut down. The best part is that no one will suspect that you had any involvement. It will be our patsy who does the dirty work."

Seamus folded his arms, leaned back in his chair, and contemplated the ceiling as he considered Collins' proposition. Mickey waited impatiently for his boss to think through the pros and cons of the plan. After just a few minutes, Seamus resumed his original position and graced Mickey with a slow, malicious, grin.

"Do it."

Chapter 6

"All right, Monty, try that again. I don't think he's coming through his back enough." Lionel smiled to himself as Monty tried to hide his dissatisfaction with the instruction. Today, Lionel was putting Monty and Beau through some basic dressage exercises to both improve Beau's back and hindquarters strength and Monty's sensitivity to Beau's mouth through contact on the bit.

"We've been working on basics forever, Lionel," Monty complained. "Can't we do something more fun for a while? There's a fence right over there we can pop over with no trouble at all."

"Not until you give me a three loop serpentine with proper bend, and keep Beau on the bit throughout," Lionel called. He watched the pair closely as Monty competently executed the movement.

"Good. Now for your reward, take Beau over the two intermediate fences at the end of the arena. He should enjoy that."

"So will I," Monty called over his shoulder. "Just watch." Lionel watched at first with curiosity then in disbelief as Monty aimed Beau at the two fences, then when he was lined up correctly, dropped the reins and spread his arms out to his sides as if he were flying. Beau seemed to not even notice there wasn't anyone at the other end of the reins, because he took both fences effortlessly. Monty remained solidly in the saddle, a huge grin spreading across his face.

Lionel knew he should be furious with the man, but he had spent enough time with both Monty and Beau to know that they were perfectly capable of handling intermediate fences with little effort, that dressage bored both of them, and that they needed this release as a reward for their patience in humoring him in this aspect of the training. Not to mention the fact that Monty's spirited nature and pure enjoyment of riding stirred something deep within Lionel he thought had died with Nigel. Pure, honest affection, and, even more problematic, sexual attraction.

After that fateful day two months ago when Monty Campbell had entered their lives, matters regarding Gideon's Rainbow's status as a prospective mount for the British National Equestrian Team had progressed with speed. Lionel had negotiated an acceptable lease agreement with the Team, establishing Monty and Beau as a competitive pair, and it hadn't taken long before the two of them made their presence known on the international jumping circuit.

As for Lionel himself, his vow to keep his relationship with Monty on a strictly professional level was becoming more and more difficult to keep. As he worked with Beau and Monty on an almost daily basis in training, his physical attraction to Monty become more difficult to mask, and, to make matters worse, Monty had shown himself to be a much more complicated man than he had initially appeared.

When Lionel had teased Monty about his frequent calls home to his mother, Monty had taken the time to explain the situation with his brother Gavin, and that he was calling to keep track of his progress in rehab. Monty then went on to explain that he was sending the majority of his winnings on the circuit home to help pay for Gavin's treatment, and Lionel's admiration for the man grew exponentially. As a result, Lionel had grown to admire the man not only for his physique but for his character, and that was proving to be dangerous to his composure.

During their training sessions, Lionel quickly discovered that Monty was a truly exceptional rider. Time after time, when Beau grew bored with a particular training exercise and challenged him, he exhibited an intuitive sensitivity as a rider that Lionel grew to admire and appreciate, as did Beau. Any clashes between Beau and Monty grew fewer and further between as they worked together. Over the past few weeks, they had bonded as a team that had proven to be nearly unbeatable in competition. In just a few days, Monty and Beau would be competing in the Longines Global Champions Tour event in Prague.

AS IN THE MAJORITY of their recent outings, Prague had been a successful competition for the pair, as they were one of only 5 horse/rider combinations to make the jump-off.

Lionel watched Monty and Beau enter the jump course and tried desperately to keep himself calm. His gaze was immediately drawn to Monty, who, with his dark auburn hair and tall, erect figure, stood out in stark relief from the other competitors. *Be still my heart.* Lionel knew he had to keep his emotions in check as Monty cantered Beau slowly around the perimeter as they waited for the timekeeper to signal them it was time to begin their final jump-off round.

The arena grew quiet as Monty was given the signal, and he guided Beau toward the first jump. The crowd held its collective breath, as this first jump was considered one of the most difficult on the course, but Beau sailed over with ease and was already eagerly looking for the next jump. It didn't take long to see that this big bay horse and his rider were a cut above the rest.

Beau approached each jump with eager anticipation, and Monty confidently steered the gelding through the very difficult course in record time. When they finished their round two seconds faster than the previous leader, the crowd roared their approval. True to form, Monty waved enthusiastically to the crowd and gave Beau's gracefully arched neck a couple of firm pats of reward for a job well done as they cantered toward the exit.

Grinning in relief and pride, Lionel rushed to meet them there.

"Well done, Monty, indeed, very well done!" Lionel went to shake Monty's hand and fought to contain his physical reaction as Monty grinned and grasped his hand in a warm, firm grip.

"Thank you, Lionel." Had Lionel detected a hitch in Monty's voice? Could he be feeling the same jolt of attraction? "I couldn't have done it without this spectacular horse of yours." He dismounted and handed the reins to Rachel, who was standing close by. The three, along with Beau, walked slowly back to the stabling area.

"I've never ridden a horse that loved to jump as much as this one. He truly craves the spotlight. I know you've seen it too."

"I have. Beau has always been that way. He visibly changes into another horse when in competition. He somehow gets bigger and stronger—more confident and energetic. It's a bit frightening to experience if you don't expect it, because he's so laid back at home."

As if he knew he was being discussed and complimented, Beau nodded his head and snorted his agreement. Lionel grinned at the gelding and patted his neck. "You cheeky bastard! You know we're talking about you, don't you?"

Monty grinned as well, and the two men's gazes collided. Lionel caught his breath as he saw a flash of desire cross Monty's face before he quickly masked it. So, Monty did return his attraction. The question was, was Lionel ready to do something about it? Could he handle taking their relationship to the next level? How would Monty react? Lionel's mind spun with the possibilities, and his body reacted, his face flushed, and his breath increased.

Then a flash of guilt intruded. What was he thinking? Even if Monty returned his affections, a relationship between them would be detrimental to Monty's career. As soon as the gossips then the press got word that they were more than mere acquaintances, his sordid past would be dragged up, and Monty would suffer. He couldn't do that to him just as he was reaching the height of his potential. *No, this can't happen.*

Lionel got his emotions under control and cooled his attitude, quickly turning away from Monty. "Let's get Beau away from the crowd while the rest of the riders go. We can cool him down now but won't be able to put him away yet. After your performance today, I'm certain you'll be back to get your ribbon, trophy, and cheque for the Championship."

~ ~ ~

"Sure. No problem. Thanks." Monty noticed Lionel's sudden coolness and was at a loss to understand what had happened. Unable to think of what he might have said to trigger such a reaction, he dismissed his feeling as oversensitivity after the adrenaline rush had just come down from. He quickly dismounted and together with Lionel led the gelding back away from the crowd to wait for the rest of the riders to finish. Rachel came forward with a cooler for Beau and after placing it on the gelding, began to walk him slowly around the warm-up area, in anticipation of the upcoming award presentation.

Chapter 7

The award ceremony had gone without a hitch, and after bidding Lionel and Rachel a good evening, Monty was relaxing in the stabling area prior to returning to the hotel. He reviewed the events of the day and recalled especially how Lionel had looked. The expression of pride mixed with a hint of desire on the man's face made him want to burst. *Careful, man, that's exactly how Archie looked at you right before he informed you he wasn't really that interested in anything more than a brief fling.*

Monty's heart turned cold at the recollection of the trainer he had naively fallen in love with. Monty had only been twenty-one years old when his trusted trainer, Archie Morrison, ten years his senior, seduced him by leading him to believe he loved him, then callously dumped him when another young buck caught his eye. Monty had been devastated. His heart broken. From that day on, he had resolved never to allow another man to have the power to break his heart.

But Lionel isn't anything like Archie. Monty had to admit that Lionel had never attempted to take their relationship beyond that of trainer and rider, but he resolved that this was not the time to enter a personal relationship with his horse's trainer. Life was complicated enough for now.

He heard a soft nicker, and looked over at Beau, who was looking at him with what Monty could swear was a smug look of superiority on his face. "Proud of yourself, eh?" Monty asked with a grin. Beau snorted and nodded emphatically. "Cheeky bloke. You really can understand us." He moved to give the gelding a well-deserved treat when suddenly, a loud shout broke the companionable silence.

"Yo, Campbell!"

Monty turned in the direction of the shout and saw another member of the British team, David Morris, striding down the barn aisle toward him.

"Morris, what are you doing here at this late hour?"

"I was hoping I could find someone to help me," Morris said, relief evident in his voice. "I need a second opinion. My horse has been feeling a bit off the past couple of days, but neither I nor the team vet can find anything wrong. Do you mind looking?"

"Of course I don't mind." Monty then noticed how quickly darkness had fallen. "It's getting a bit late to do anything tonight. We'd have a hard time seeing much in the dark. Why don't I meet you here tomorrow morning early, and we can watch him together and see if we can see anything?"

David flashed Monty a grateful smile. "Sounds like a plan. Thank you so much."

"No problem. See you in the morning."

THE NEXT MORNING, LIONEL met Rachel in the hotel lobby. "Have you seen Monty this morning?" Lionel asked. "No. I haven't seen him since we left the stabling area last night. He said he wanted to stay there for a while and decompress after the excitement of yesterday."

"Right." Lionel went to the desk clerk and asked if he'd seen Mr. Campbell this morning.

"Yes, sir, as a matter of fact, I did. He left about an hour ago with another gentleman. They appeared to be wearing riding clothes."

"Then he must be back at the competition grounds," Rachel said. "Let's go see what he's up to and get Beau ready to transport back home."

"Agreed," Lionel said, his curiosity piqued. What was Monty doing with another man, and why was he wearing riding clothes? The competition was over, and most of the competitors were packing up and preparing to leave the area.

When they arrived in the stabling area, Lionel scanned the surrounds for any sight of Monty. He soon saw the tall, auburn-haired young man riding a horse Lionel didn't recognize, and as he rode at a comfortable canter, Monty spoke seriously with another man, who was standing on the ground within a couple of meters of the horse.

They were both concerned about something, but from this distance, Lionel couldn't make out the conversation. Suddenly, without warning, the horse's hind legs seemed to simply collapse underneath it, and both horse and rider went down hard to the ground.

"Oh my God!" Rachel exclaimed, and Lionel, whose heart was in his throat, started running full speed toward the scene all the while praying that Monty was safe.

"Monty! Monty! Are you all right?" The man who had been with Monty was kneeling next to him, trying as best he could to pull him out of the way of the thrashing hooves of the now-struggling horse.

"Get out of my way!" Lionel exclaimed as he elbowed his way past the closely packed group of onlookers that had appeared seemingly out of nowhere to see if he could assist. He saw that Monty was still lying down, but appeared to be conscious, although he would need to see a doctor. The horse had finally gotten up, and was led away, visibly limping and still trembling from the experience.

Lionel knelt near Monty's head. "Monty, can you hear me?" Lionel's voice shook with fear as he desperately waited for Monty to respond.

Monty looked in the direction of Lionel's voice, found his face, and tried to give him a reassuring smile. Unfortunately, what Lionel saw was more of a grimace than a smile, although he was encouraged that Monty was able to focus on him. Lionel also sent a silent prayer of thanks that Monty was wearing a helmet. If he hadn't been, his injuries would have been much worse.

"Lionel, what are you doing here?" Monty croaked. "Never mind that, what are you doing riding a crippled horse?"

The man who had apparently owned the horse Monty had been riding responded. "He was doing me a favor, Mr. Hayes. My horse had been acting strangely and I didn't know what was wrong with him. Monty offered to help me figure out what the problem was. I had no idea the issue was that severe. I'm so sorry."

Monty had been listening to the conversation and started to get up. "Not to worry, David. I'm all right. Nothing broken—at least not that I can tell."

"You're going to the hospital right now, and I'll have no argument," Lionel declared. "I'll take you myself."

"Lionel, it's not necessary. I've fallen off horses before, you know. I can tell if I have a serious injury." Monty slowly stood and gingerly brushed the dust off his breeches and polo shirt. He made a show of moving his arms and legs to demonstrate to Lionel that everything was functioning as it should.

"See, everything's fine. I'm bruised but not broken."

"Only because you're the luckiest bastard I've ever met," Lionel said grudgingly. "Any other man would be unconscious or worse after a fall like that. You're lucky the horse didn't fall on top of you."

At that moment, Rachel appeared, and Monty again attempted reassure her that everything was all right. Lionel looked Monty over once again and wasn't happy with what he saw.

"I don't care what you say, you need to go to the hospital to make sure there are no internal injuries. That was a nasty fall."

Monty sighed. "All right, I'll go, but I want you to take me. No ambulances."

"Agreed."

Lionel assured Rachel that he could handle Monty and left her at the showgrounds to begin preparations to transport Beau. He then led Monty carefully to his car. As they drove to the nearest hospital, Lionel looked over at Monty and remembered how he had felt when he saw the horse Monty was riding collapse underneath him like a puppet whose strings had been cut. To say he had been terrified didn't begin to cover the range of emotions he had gone through in that moment. For now, he found the best way of coping was to get things under control and keep busy so he didn't have to relive the moment over and over in his head.

Once they got to the hospital, the doctors and nurses took over. Thankfully, a few spoke some English, and it was relatively easy to communicate exactly what had happened. Monty was taken to an examination room, and Lionel was left in the waiting room for the moment while they did their examinations.

The smell of antiseptic permeated the room, and there was a television in the corner blaring what appeared to be a talk show in Czech. The vinyl-padded chairs were less than comfortable, and the ugly green linoleum flooring reminded him of his mother's pea soup—not a pleasant memory. *How do people spend hours waiting in this hellish room?*

Lionel quickly found he couldn't just sit there and wait, so he stood and paced the floor, his mind racing. As he relived the moments that led to them being here in the hospital, Lionel's fear gradually morphed into anger. How could Monty put himself at risk like that? Didn't he understand how important he was to Lionel, and to Rachel and Beau as well?

What would Lionel do if Monty were killed? He could never survive losing him. Didn't he understand that? *Wait, what?* Lionel caught himself before his thoughts could go any further, but he had to acknowledge that he didn't feel a bit of remorse or guilt when he accepted how important Monty had become to him. His fury at Monty for taking the risk, however, only increased as his imagination came up with a myriad of potential consequences Monty had averted only by dumb luck.

At that moment, Monty appeared, a doctor by his side. Lionel approached the two men, and extended a hand to the doctor, whose name tag indicated he was Dr. Koryta. The doctor shook Lionel's hand with a firm grip.

"Mr. Hayes, I'm pleased to meet you." He looked at Monty briefly then returned his attention to Lionel.

Upon seeing Monty again, now with his cuts and scrapes bandaged and walking with a noticeable limp, Lionel struggled to get his emotions under control. He schooled himself to be as neutral as possible in front of the doctor, who was a stranger to them. The result was that his voice was cold and detached. He was still livid at Monty for taking such a stupid risk, but he would deal with Monty properly once he had him alone.

"What's the diagnosis, Doctor? Is there anything we need to know before I take him out of here?"

The doctor spoke in a heavily accented English, but Lionel was able to understand him. "Ideally, I'd like to keep Mr. Campbell here for observation, but he insists that he is fine and wants to leave with you. In that case, although Mr. Campbell doesn't show any indications of a concussion, I recommend he be watched for twenty-four hours to ensure he doesn't exhibit any signs or symptoms of concussion. Look for any instances of severe headache, dizziness, confusion, lack of ability to concentrate, or any other behavior that is out of the ordinary. If he exhibits any of those symptoms, please bring him back here, or to another hospital immediately."

Lionel spared a glance at Monty. Although still a bit more pale than usual, he appeared to be all right, and capable of leaving under his own power. Fine, if he wanted to leave, Lionel would go along, but he was still going to read Monty the riot act about his recklessness, concussion or not.

As the two left the hospital, Monty asked about Rachel and Beau.

"Rachel went ahead and prepped Beau for transport back to the UK. She will accompany him there and wait for me to call with a status report. I'll be taking you to your hotel room, and, as the doctor required, I'll be staying there to watch you for twenty-four hours."

Monty sighed. "Lionel, you don't have to do that. The doctor didn't even confirm I'd had a concussion, and I think they're being overly cautious just to protect themselves. I'm fine."

They both got into Lionel's car, and Lionel used the GPS to get them to their hotel. The silence in the car was filled with tension. Neither man wanted to start a conversation, each implicitly understanding that nothing could be said at that moment to diffuse the situation.

When they arrived at the hotel, Lionel stopped at the front desk briefly to inform the staff that they would be staying for another night, possibly two.

Chapter 8

When Monty heard Lionel reserve a room for another two nights, he rolled his eyes, although he made sure that Lionel didn't see his reaction. It appeared Lionel didn't believe him when he said that he was fine, and that he didn't have a concussion. Well, if what Lionel had said in the car was true, and he would be spending at least the next 24 hours with him, maybe he could make the most of the time.

When they got to Monty's room, Lionel took the key and opened the door. The room had been made up while they were gone, and Monty's belongings were mostly packed, obviously in anticipation of them leaving this day to go back home. Monty, who after several weeks in close contact with Lionel had become sensitive to the man's every mood, had felt the tension flowing from him ever since they left the hospital. He knew the man was a powder keg waiting to go off. Sure enough, as soon as Lionel closed the door behind him and dropped his luggage, he faced Monty, his face contorted in anger.

"What in the hell were you thinking, getting on that fucking horse?" Lionel shouted. "You realize you could have been catastrophically injured, or even killed?"

Monty flinched in the face of Lionel's admittedly justifiable anger. Yet he was his own man and was perfectly capable of making his own decisions. He did not have to answer to anyone, including Lionel, for the choices he made. At the same time, however, he knew that there was nothing he could say at this moment that would mollify Lionel.

It was probably better to just let him get this anger and frustration out of his system. Then, they could have a civilized conversation. Still, Lionel's question begged for an answer. Monty did his best to provide one that wouldn't provoke the man further.

"It's like David told you—the horse was merely off, not crippled. He had even had his vet look at the horse, and the vet found nothing. Neither of us had any idea the horse was going to collapse like that. Believe me, Lionel, if I had known that there was damage to that horse's spine, I would not have gotten on him." Monty found himself working to suppress the sudden surge of anger he himself was feeling at Lionel's obvious lack of confidence in his ability to judge horseflesh or people.

Seeming at least a bit mollified, Lionel backed off and appeared to relax from the tension he had been holding. He ran his fingers through his hair in a gesture Monty knew to be a sign he was fighting frustration. "I know you have experience with horses, but you're not a vet." He moved closer and reached out to grasp Monty's shoulder and give it a squeeze. He looked the young Scot directly in his eyes, his gaze as serious as Monty had ever seen. His voice was choked with emotion. "Do you have any idea how terrified I was when I saw that horse go down with you?"

The sincerity in Lionel's gaze caused warmth to spread through Monty's chest. His heart swelled, and he could barely breathe at the thought that Lionel might care about him that much. His eyes filled with tears at the enormity of his feelings for this man. There was no way he could resist the magnetic pull he had felt for Lionel since the first day they met.

"Lionel, I'm so sorry," he choked through the lump in his throat. He reached out to Lionel, cupped his face in his hands and used his thumbs to wipe away the tears that had begun to fall down his face. "I had no idea my welfare mattered so much to you. It will never happen again." It was difficult to say which of them closed the distance between them first, but before either of them was aware, their lips were locked in a fiery kiss, and neither seemed eager to come up for air.

It wasn't long before articles of clothing were being ripped from bodies until they were both completely naked. Lionel paused for a moment to step back and look at Monty's nude form. He visibly winced at the angry red, purple, and blue bruises that had resulted from the fall.

"My God, even all banged up, you're gorgeous!" Lionel gazed hungrily over Monty's lean, muscular body. Monty grew self-conscious when Lionel's gaze lingered over the bruises on Monty's ribs, elbows, hips, and thighs, which likely served as a reminder to Lionel that he would have to take it easy on Monty because of his very recent fall.

To distract Lionel from his injuries and turn matters back to seduction, Monty moved closer to Lionel, took his face in his hands, and began kissing him passionately. He then slowly trailed kisses down Lionel's neck and chest, lingering at his nipples long enough to suckle them gently, then nip and caress them with his tongue.

His tactics appeared to work as Lionel moaned with pleasure and drew back from Monty long enough to focus for a few seconds on Monty's flat, defined stomach, then stopped for an even longer time to gaze at his long, thick cock jutting out from a nest of dark-auburn curls. Lionel grinned at the sight, then groaned again as his own cock twitched with desire.

Lionel's heated inspection only made Monty more aroused than he had already been. Since turnabout was fair play, Monty took the opportunity to scan Lionel's long, lean body as well, noticing the light-blond fur on his chest, which tapered to a narrow trail down his flat stomach, and ended in a nest for his narrow, but enticingly long cock, also jutting proudly upward, his arousal clearly evident.

Monty's hands then slowly followed the trail his eyes had first tread, and he finished by grasping Lionel's cock firmly, stroking it, then cupping his balls.

At Lionel's quick intake of breath, Monty licked his lips in anticipation, and Lionel groaned in response. He had clearly figured out what Monty had in mind. Monty grinned, fell to his knees and took Lionel's cock into his hot, wet mouth. As the head of Lionel's cock met the back of his throat, Monty looked up into Lionel's eyes and swallowed around him.

"Bloody hell, yes!" Lionel cried, leaning back a little so as not to cause Monty to gag. Undeterred, Monty grabbed Lionel's ass cheeks and pulled him back into his throat again. He sucked and twirled and licked until finally allowing Lionel to draw back and give them both a break.

"You look so beautiful with my cock in your mouth," Lionel whispered in awe. "You are the most beautiful man I've ever seen."

Monty smiled in response, and made to return to sucking Lionel's cock, when Lionel raised him up and drew him slowly toward the bed. Monty followed, his curiosity piqued. When they were both lying on the bed, Lionel positioned himself so that he was on his hands and knees over Monty with his mouth over Monty's cock. Lionel's cock was similarly positioned over Monty's mouth.

"Ah, sixty-nine, one of my favorites," Monty said in appreciation.

"This way, all you have to do is lie there and let me pleasure you, and I will do the same."

Monty grinned in response. "Sounds lovely. What are we waiting for?"

Monty used one hand to guide Lionel's cock back into his mouth, while caressing his balls with the other, then used his tongue, lips and throat to pleasure him.

From the sounds Lionel was making, he was succeeding. It appeared, however, that Lionel took it as a challenge to use his skillful mouth to see if he could make Monty come first, but ultimately, among a chorus of ecstatic moans, they both climaxed almost simultaneously.

After a few moments of satisfied afterglow, Lionel moved to position himself next to his lover, and Monty curled himself around Lionel's body, wrapping his arms around him in a gesture of gratitude and comfort. He smiled to himself as he drifted off to sleep. *I don't think I've ever been this happy.*

Chapter 9

Lionel woke up to a feeling of warmth and comfort he had not felt in ages. As he attempted to move, he realized that he couldn't—he was surrounded by warm, strong arms, and his legs were pinned between long, muscular legs. A deliciously sweet mouth was gently laying soft kisses on the back of his neck and shoulders. His eager cock instantly responded, and Lionel allowed himself a moment of pure happiness before coming back completely into reality. *What have I done?*

Monty must have felt Lionel's body tense, because he ceased his amorous attentions and moved away enough to allow Lionel to turn onto his back. Monty propped on an elbow, his head in his hand, and looked Lionel squarely in the eye.

"What's wrong, love?" His voice held a bit of a tremor, and his expression was one of dread, as if he expected Lionel to reject him outright. *Bollocks on that.* As if he could ever reject this man after what they had shared over the past few weeks, and especially after last night. What was the answer? Lionel racked his brain, but nothing feasible came immediately to mind.

Lionel reached up and brushed a wayward lock of thick, auburn hair away from Monty's brilliant blue eyes. "It's all right, sweetheart. I'm OK. It's just that I'm worried about how this thing between us will impact your reputation. You know I'm not totally clean in the eyes of the establishment. Even after all this time without a hint of trouble. Any association with me will raise questions. I care about you more than you can imagine, but we can't be seen together. Not as a couple anyway."

Lionel avoided the look of pain that had appeared in Monty's eyes, and slowly left the bed, collected his clothes and made his way to the shower to prepare for the day. He could sense Monty's gaze focused directly on him, knowing that there was so much more that needed to be said. He only wished he knew what.

"Don't walk away from me, Lionel. Not now." Lionel could hear a hint of desperation in Monty's voice. It was as if Monty knew if he let Lionel leave him now, they would never be able to return to this place in their relationship.

Lionel turned and faced Monty; his own anguish apparent. "What would you have me do?" He slashed his hand through the air. "Wave a magic wand, and make my past go away?" He laughed harshly. "Believe me, if that were possible, I would have done it a long time ago. I have paid an enormous price for one mistake, and still they won't let me forget it." He turned and resumed his walk to the shower, his shoulders slumped in defeat.

Monty's heart broke at the sight of this once vital and extraordinary man laid low by a situation he was powerless to change. He wanted so much to hold Lionel and comfort him, but he knew any gesture he would make would only make things worse. If only there was something he could do. At that moment, the telephone in his room rang, and when he answered, his mother was on the line. Monty's first reaction was fear. His mother hardly ever called him when he was out of the country competing. "Hello, Ma. Is everything OK? How is Gavin?"

"Everything's fine with Gavin, sweetheart. He's doing so well that they're going to move him from the rehab center to an outpatient facility nearby. But that's not why I'm calling. I heard you had an accident at the showgrounds yesterday. Are you all right?"

Monty was amazed at how quickly word of his mishap had spread, but then again, there were people with cellphones at the competition grounds, and it was certain that someone had taken a video of his fall.

If that was the case, then it was a given that with his fame on the show circuit, people would be interested in seeing anything newsworthy about him. A catastrophic fall would be everywhere on social media.

"I'm fine, Ma. Just a few bruises. Nothing major, although Lionel did take me to the hospital to make sure I was OK."

"I like Lionel. He seems to be a good man." Monty smiled to himself. It appeared his mother was attempting to match make for him. *Not to worry, Ma, I'm way ahead of you.*

"He is that, Ma. A very good man. I like him a lot." He hoped that his mother would get the message and leave him alone. In the past she had been somewhat heavy handed in her attempts to find him a partner. It appeared she believed him, because, to Monty's relief, she immediately changed the subject.

"You'll be happy to know that Gavin has finished his treatment at the rehab facility in Aberdeen. Your father and I visited him there yesterday, and he was in very good spirits. They will be sending him to a halfway house in London, which will be the next step in his recovery. They think that's best since he will be far away from the friends that had such a bad influence on him to begin with.

As soon as we know more, we'll be sure to let you know. And, Monty, thank you so much for sending us the money to pay for his treatment. We never would have been able to afford to place him there without it."

"I'm glad I could do it, Ma. What are my winnings for if not to help support my family when they're in need? If Beau and I continue to perform well, we'll have even more money if Gavin needs additional help."

"That's wonderful news, son. Thank you so much. Take care, and call when you can."

"I will, Ma. Goodbye."

A few minutes later, Monty's mother called to let him know that Gavin would be in Room 1231 at the halfway house in London. After he thanked his mother for the information and hung up, Monty laid back against the pillows and closed his eyes, taking a deep, cleansing breath. At least one thing in his life was working well. Gavin in recovery was a wonderful result after all those years of anguish. Monty knew the statistics about relapse, and that it was all too common, but Gavin was strong. If he made his mind up, he could beat this addiction. Monty was certain.

Chapter 10

Monty found himself again standing on the winners' podium—this time at the Longines Masters in Lausanne, Switzerland. Even as the crowd was cheering, and as show officials were presenting each of the top three finishers their trophies and Longines watches, Monty scanned the crowd for a glimpse of Lionel. He quickly found his lover standing toward the back of the crowd, with huge smile on his face, clearly enjoying another triumph.

Beau had again put in a spectacular performance, and it seemed everyone who was anyone in the British equestrian world were finally taking notice. According to Lionel's friend Michael Stafford, the papers back home were trumpeting their triumph, although a few of the more tabloid- like publications were determined to bring up Lionel's past. Damn them for dredging up the entire shameful incident. Lionel did not deserve to be dragged through the mud for something that happened over two years ago.

Monty grinned, smiled and waved to Lionel, then looked over at Rachel, who had just taken Beau from him after he dismounted to his take his place as winner on the podium. She also seemed to be smiling as she spoke quietly to Beau and walked him in a small circle to calm him in the face of the boisterous crowd of avid fans.

I've never been this happy. What can I possibly have done to deserve all of this? Monty was suddenly overcome by a feeling of dread. Maybe it was the memory of his Scots grandfather who often said in moments of triumph, "Always remember, lad, *they that dance must pay the fiddler,*" that was causing this sudden bad feeling. Monty visibly shook himself to revive his good spirits. He sought out Lionel again and flashed him a mischievous wink. Lionel winked in return. Yes, things were going to be all right.

After a brief celebration involving a bottle of champagne and some decadent Swiss chocolate back at the stables, Lionel and Monty left Rachel to feed and bed down Beau.

"Don't do anything I wouldn't do, boys," she called after them with a cheeky grin.

"That leaves us a lot of options, darling," Lionel shot back, the laughter in his voice softening the obvious insult.

Both men laughed heartily as Rachel playfully flashed them her middle finger, then arm in arm, they headed back to the hotel. At Lionel's insistence, they both maintained separate rooms, but every night, after the activity in the hotel ceased, Lionel made his way to Monty's room, where they spent the night making love and talking about anything and everything. Tonight was no exception.

"What was going through your mind the night you decided to give Accolade the drug?" As soon as he asked the question, Monty wished he could take it back. The look of anguish on Lionel's face was enough to cause Monty to feel a similar pain as well. "Never mind, that was a terrible question to ask. Forget I asked."

"No, it's all right," Lionel tried to reassure him. "I want you to know, so you don't make the same mistake I did." He turned in the bed to face Monty and described the events of that night. It didn't surprise Monty at all that even though he knew Lionel wished he could forget that night, the events stayed vivid in his memory.

"So, now that you've had a chance to look back, was your decision to drug Accolade justified?"

Lionel sighed. "No. It wasn't. I've had a lot of time to think about my actions back then, I realize now that it wasn't Accolade that wasn't good enough. It was me. If I had believed in myself more, and not allowed my feelings of self-doubt to take over, I would have realized that Accolade wasn't the problem at all. It was my subconscious belief in my inability to ride him to his best that sabotaged my perception."

"At the time, however, I couldn't acknowledge even to myself that my riding actually was good enough. That it was my warped perception of my riding that was the problem. My downfall came when I couldn't admit that to myself and ended up blaming Accolade instead—even though in hindsight, and from what others tell me now, he was performing admirably."

Monty was impressed that Lionel had taken responsibility for his actions and had done the work to figure out how he had gotten to that point. He doubted he could do the same, although he had a feeling there was still more that Lionel hadn't revealed to him.

"Thank you for sharing that with me, Lionel. I know it had to be difficult, and if it makes any difference, I think I understand what you must have been going through. I have the utmost admiration for you taking responsibility and doing the hard work to discover what was at the heart of the issue."

Lionel made a self-deprecating snort. "I have Nigel to thank for most of those insights. He and I talked *ad nauseum* about my true motivations for doing what I did. Believe me, I didn't come by this insight easily or quickly. Thank God the dear man stuck with me, though. I don't know where I would be today without him. I'll never forget him."

Monty watched as Lionel fought to swallow back tears when he thought about Nigel, and everything the two of them had gone through. It was as if Lionel had taken a knife and stabbed him in the heart. *He still loves him. I may have his body, but I'll never have a chance to win his heart.*

Chapter 11

Monty realized that Lionel had noticed his distress and was visibly withdrawing—misinterpreting his reaction as a rejection. He needed to reassure Lionel that assumption was wrong as quickly as possible. He reached out and took Lionel's hand in his own.

"I can sympathize with your sense of loss, Lionel. Nigel was a very special man, and everyone who knew him admired him. They also without exception praised your relationship as one of mutual respect and abiding love. I simply can't imagine how that must feel."

Lionel's countenance could not have looked more nonplussed. It seemed Monty's explanation was the last thing Lionel had expected. After a moment, seeming to have nothing further to say, he quickly changed the subject.

"Look, why don't I take a shower, and let you have some time alone. Maybe you should call your mother and find out how Gavin is doing at the halfway house."

Monty brightened at the suggestion. "Great idea. You go ahead, and I'll do just that."

Just as Lionel shut the bathroom door and started the water in the shower, Monty's cell phone rang. Maybe his mother had been reading his mind and saved him a call. When he looked at the display, however, the caller ID showed 'Unknown Caller' which confused Monty. Maybe it was a telemarketer?

"Hello?"

"Monty Campbell?" The voice on the other end of the

line was muffled, and clearly disguised.

"Yes, this is Monty Campbell. Who is this?"

"Let's just say I'm a friend concerned for the welfare of your brother, Gavin."

Monty's heart constricted in his chest. He fought to breathe as he sensed a threat in the man's voice. "What about Gavin? Is he OK?"

"He is now, but he may not stay that way unless you do exactly as I tell you."

Monty's fear quickly morphed in anger. "Is this some kind of joke? Who are you and what do you want? You must know that if you harm my brother in any way, I'll find you and make sure you're brought to justice."

"Let me assure you, I'm not joking. At this very moment, your brother is in a halfway house in London, and he is in Room 1231. Does that information sound familiar to you?"

Monty's heart skipped a beat. "How did you get that information?"

"That's not important. What is important is that you must agree to follow my instructions to the letter. If you do, then your brother will be fine. If you don't comply, I will make sure your brother receives enough heroine laced with fentanyl to ensure he dies within seconds. Nothing will be able to save him. Am I clear?"

Monty tried to swallow past the enormous lump in his throat. His heart was beating a hundred miles an hour as he tried to get a grip on his emotions. He needed to keep his wits about him if he was going to save Gavin's life, and that's exactly what this man was threatening, in no uncertain terms. He looked to the bathroom and could still hear the shower running. *Good. Lionel should be none the wiser about whatever this is.* He then turned his attention back to the mysterious caller.

"Yes. I understand. What is it exactly that you want me to do?"

The voice on the other end chuckled. "It's actually quite easy, Mr. Campbell. All you have to do is take the syringe and vial of serum that we've secreted in your suitcase, and plant it in Gideon's Rainbow's traveling first-aid kit."

"You've put something in my bag? When did you do that? How?" Monty scrambled off the bed and opened his suitcase. He rummaged around until he found a flat leather pouch. He opened the pouch, which was just big enough to hold a medical syringe and vial of liquid. Monty recognized the substance named on the label of the vial as a drug banned for use on horses competing in international, FEI-sanctioned competitions.

A cold feeling of dread spread through his body, and his hand shook with the enormity of the implications this vial raised both for himself, and especially for Lionel. There was only one reason why someone would want this drug planted on a horse trained by Lionel Hayes, and the fact that this unknown attacker would use him as the instrument of his attack and probably get away with it was more than he could bear.

"Why are you doing this? Lionel Hayes is a good man. He doesn't deserve to be ruined like this. That's what you're trying to do, isn't it? Ruin Lionel Hayes? At least tell me that much. As the tool you're using to destroy Lionel, I think I deserve to know."

"You deserve nothing," the voice stated. "Just plant the evidence, and we'll do the rest. If you're lucky, Hayes will never know it was you that planted the drug."

Yes, but even if he never finds out, I'll know, and I'll never be able to live with myself if I do this. But what choice did he have? They had access to Gavin and could murder him and easily make it look like just another junkie relapsing and dying of an overdose. No one would ever know there had been foul play.

Monty felt sorrow deeper than any he had ever experienced when he realized that if he wanted to save his brother, he would have to sacrifice the man he loved. Yes, he could admit to himself that he loved Lionel more than he had ever loved another man. Why was it only just now, when he would be required to destroy the man to save his only brother that he could finally admit his true feelings?

He responded to the man in the only way he could. His voice flat, devoid of emotion. "All right. I'll do it."

"Good. You need to plant the drug as soon as possible. Once that's done, you will call the number I'm texting to you now and leave a message letting us know the drug is in place. We'll do the rest. You've done the right thing, Campbell. Hayes doesn't deserve your loyalty."

You don't know him at all if you believe that. "I'll do as you say, but I'll not take any pleasure in it. I need your word that Gavin will be safe."

"If you do exactly as we require, no harm will come to your brother. You have my word."

The word of a criminal. Faint hope, that. At that moment, a text message appeared on his phone with a telephone number. So, all was in place. All he had to do was plant the evidence that would frame Lionel for another incident of illegal drugging and ruin his life forever. He looked to the heavens and sighed, his heart heavy with grief. *Please, God, there must be a way out of this. Help me. I don't know what to do.*

Chapter 12

The following morning dawned rainy, unseasonably cold, and dreary—which matched Monty's emotional state perfectly. Yesterday, after the fateful phone call, it took everything Monty had to school his features and demeanor so Lionel wouldn't suspect the emotional turmoil roiling just beneath the surface.

Since his desperate plea to the Almighty yesterday, divine providence had not intervened to provide Monty with a solution to his problem. Try as he might, he couldn't come up with a foolproof way to protect both Lionel and Gavin without hurting one of them, likely killing his brother outright.

In Lionel's case, an injury to his reputation wouldn't be fatal. True, if Lionel's reputation were sullied by a drugging scandal a second time, his career, if not his life with horses entirely, would be forever ruined, but ultimately he would be still be alive.

That fact was what Monty latched onto as the solution to his dilemma. He would have to plant the drug. The best he could hope for was that that Lionel wouldn't know it was Monty that had done the deed. If Lionel didn't know, once the inevitable scandal hit, Monty would be able to support Lionel, to be there to love him and comfort him and even support him financially as a partner so that the consequences of the discovery of the drug would not be so devastating. Lionel would be ruined, but with Monty's love he would live, and, Monty hoped, someday be accepted again.

The pouch with the syringe and vial of illegal steroid was sitting in his right-hand jacket pocket, making its toxic presence known every time he stuffed his hands in his pockets to warm them. With a sense of foreboding, he walked toward the stabling area where Rachel was directing the grooms to pack up all their belongings and get Beau ready for transport. He looked around, and when it appeared no one was looking in his direction, he removed the pouch from his pocket and lifted the lid of Beau's tack trunk so that he could put the damaging materials inside.

"Hello, love. Is everything going as planned?"

Monty jumped in surprise, and as he spun to see Lionel standing immediately behind him, the pouch fell from his hand onto the floor between Monty and Lionel.

"What's this?" Lionel bent down, picked up the pouch, and examined it closely, then made to open it.

"Wait, Lionel," Monty cautioned in a hoarse whisper. He quickly placed his hand over Lionel's to ensure the pouch wasn't opened, then he glanced furtively around, and spied a deserted tack room at the end of the aisle of stalls in which they were standing. He led Lionel to the room, then, making sure that no one was watching, he pulled Lionel in and closed the door.

"What is this? What's going on?" Lionel's face reflected his confusion and concern at Monty's strange behavior, yet underneath it all, Monty could sense Lionel trusted him. The knowledge of that trust and the fact that he was about to destroy it was like a knife to his heart. He didn't deserve Lionel's trust, and he was about to prove it in a most profound way. Now, he had no choice but to tell Lionel the truth, and hope that together they could find the answer to this untenable situation. He took the pouch from Lionel and opened it, revealing the contents.

Upon seeing the syringe and vial, then reading the label on the vial, Lionel visibly paled.

"Oh my God, Monty. What have you done?" "Nothing, Lionel. At least not yet."

Lionel's expression changed from horrified to angry in a heartbeat.

"What do you mean 'not yet'? You need to get rid of that stuff as soon as possible, or we'll both be thrown out of here on our arses and our reputations will be ruined."

Lionel started pacing within the close confines of the tack room, and Monty knew he had to do some quick explaining, or Lionel would never believe him. He reached out and grabbed Lionel by the arm to stop the pacing. He now had Lionel's complete attention. He motioned to an empty tack trunk left against the wall of the now otherwise empty room.

"Please sit down for a moment, and I can explain." Lionel nodded his agreement, and sat down on the trunk, his eyes never leaving Monty's face.

"Yesterday, while you were in the shower, I got a call on my cell from an anonymous man." Monty went on to describe in detail for Lionel the entirety of his conversation with the mysterious villain.

"Jesus, Monty. Were you really considering planting that"—he gestured wildly toward the pouch—"in Beau's tack box to frame me?"

The look of devastation on Lionel's face broke Monty's heart.

"I didn't know what to do, Lionel. The man had the number of Gavin's room at the halfway house. I didn't want him killed because of me. I love my brother.

"Gavin has been addicted to opiates since I left home to compete internationally. Without my direct influence, he started hanging out with the wrong crowd and became addicted. My parents have tried to help, but they've lost hope. It was only just recently that an almost fatal overdose awakened him to the fact that his life is at risk every time he shoots up.

"I was able to convince him to go into rehab, and my winnings were sufficient to get him into one of the best rehab facilities in Scotland, if not the entire UK. Now, he's graduated from the rehab facility to a halfway house in London. He's clean, and the thought of these people killing him using heroin as their weapon both angers and frightens me to death. I had to do something. They left me no choice."

Lionel shook his head. "But you see, Monty, you did have another choice. You could have come to me with the problem, and we could have put our heads together and found another way. Unfortunately, you didn't do that. Now, I can never trust you again."

He looked at the vial and syringe, then put them back into the pouch, and handed it back to Monty.

"If you must frame me to save your brother, then go ahead and do it. I don't want to be the man responsible for your brother's death. But be clear that when the scandal hits, and I leave here to go back home in disgrace, I never want to see you again." Lionel turned and walked out of the tack room, leaving Monty standing alone, the pouch still in his hands, his heart broken.

Chapter 13

onty stood just inside the tack room looking at the damned pouch and its contents with dread. *Now what?* Since Lionel had discovered his involvement and didn't trust him, there was no way he would accept any assistance when the scandal broke. He would be alone and truly devastated. He might even contemplate suicide. The situation had changed dramatically in just a few moments. His plan had to change, but how?

"Monty?" He looked up to see Rachel standing in the tack room doorway. Her face mirrored his own sorrow, and tears were streaming down her face. Monty reached into a back pocket of his jeans and retrieved a handkerchief, which he handed to her.

"So, how much of that did you hear?"

"All of it," she replied, her voice choked with emotion. "What are you going to do?"

"I have no idea, but I'm open to suggestions."

She straightened a bit, and her eyes started gleaming with what looked to Monty like hope.

"You know that Lionel has connections with Ian Stafford, who is former SAS. Ian has friends in the personal security business that could help you if asked." She thought a bit further, then added, "In fact, I know they would. Have you ever heard of Seamus O'Reilly and the O'Reilly crime family?

"Yes, as a matter of fact, I remember there was a big, complicated trial a few months ago where O'Reilly was found guilty of a host of crimes including murder and kidnapping. What's that got to do with this?"

"Just before last year's St Leger Stakes horse race, Ian Stafford's wife Megan was kidnapped by O'Reilly's son Ryan in an attempt to coerce Megan's father to throw the race. Ian actually had to kill Ryan O'Reilly to rescue her. Seamus vowed revenge, and ever since then Ian and Megan Stafford have hired full-time security to watch over them. They believe O'Reilly will do just about anything to get his revenge.

"It's possible that since O'Reilly can't get to Ian and Megan directly, and Michael and Jessica Stafford are in America frequently, Lionel could be an indirect target. Lionel is a good friend of Ian's brother Michael and both Ian and Michael have invested substantial sums of money in Lionel's business. If Lionel is hurt, the Staffords would be just as hurt or more. O'Reilly could easily be the source if this blackmail threat."

"So Lionel was right. If I had come to him with this first, he might have been able to help me?"

Rachel smiled weakly. "It seems so, yes."

"Do you think he'll ever forgive me?" He looked at the pouch still gripped in his hand. "You know there's no way I'm going through with this now. I don't know what I was thinking. I could never hurt Lionel like that. I love the man beyond reason."

"He loves you too, you know. That's why this is so devastating to him."

"What can I do, Rachel? He doesn't want anything to do with me, and I need him if we're going to save Gavin."

Rachel's lips turned up in a smile as she tried to give Monty a reason for optimism. "He's in shock. I don't think he's had a chance to really think this situation through. Let me talk to him. I think I can convince him to give you another chance."

Monty reached out and drew her into a hug. "Thank you, sweetheart. You're a lifesaver."

"I haven't done anything yet," she chided, "but I know he loves you, and he knows how evil O'Reilly can be. That combination might well save the day." She leaned back out of the hug and winked at Monty. "Wish me luck."

"All the luck in the world, Rachel. I'm afraid you'll need it."

She blew him a kiss and strode in the direction Lionel had taken.

Monty emptied the pouch of its contents, separated the vial and smashed it against the concrete floor, virtually destroying all evidence of illegal substance. He took a nearby shovel and broom, swept up the remains of the vial and, along with the pouch, threw it into a dumpster. He found a sharps container in the stable to dispose of the syringe. *The die is cast*, he thought to himself. Whether he likes it or not, Lionel has my brother's life in his hands.

Chapter 14

After leaving Monty, Lionel had searched for and finally found Beau. Over the time they had been together, almost from the very beginning, the gelding had been one of his favorites, and Lionel felt at home stroking the gelding's neck as he quietly informed him of his sorrow at Monty's betrayal. "I thought he loved me, Beau," Lionel confessed in a murmur no one else could hear. "I certainly loved him. How could he betray me like that?"

"Loved, past tense?" Rachel's voice appeared over his right shoulder, and he turned toward her and gave her a weak, trembling smile that didn't reach his eyes.

"Yes, sweetheart, past tense. Monty betrayed me in the worst possible way. I can never forgive or forget that."

Rachel absently stroked Beau's nose as she braced herself to make her confession.

"I know everything, Lionel. I overheard your conversation with Monty in the tack room." As Lionel's expression changed from sorrow to anger, Rachel gently grabbed Lionel's forearm to make sure he was listening to her.

"It wasn't like that. I was in the stable to make sure all of Beau's tack was in the transport and heard the two of you talking. I was going to interrupt, but then when I heard what you were discussing, I couldn't leave, nor could I interrupt to let you know I was there. Like it or not, this situation impacts me as well."

Lionel knew she was right, but he still wasn't sure he liked the fact that someone else close to him was aware of the depth of Monty's betrayal.

"So, did you see him? Did he try to win you over to his side?" Lionel began pacing, and his agitation quickly transmitted itself to Beau, who also started to walk along the paddock fence, his demeanor suddenly becoming as agitated as Lionel's.

"Lionel, please calm down. See how you're affecting Beau?"

Lionel gasped as he realized that today's scenario was very near the one that had transpired nearly two years ago at the Olympic trials. The memory of Accolade's agitation mirroring his own at the time took hold, and he winced with the memory. He took a deep breath and visibly calmed himself. The gelding quickly followed suit.

"Lionel, please listen to me. Monty loves you. He's devastated that his actions have caused you so much pain."

"He should have thought about that before he chose his brother over me," Lionel retorted.

"Do you hear what you're saying?" It was now Rachel's turn to be angry. "His brother's life was at stake. What would you expect him to do? The villain gave him a Hobson's choice. Did you really want him to sacrifice his brother's life to save your reputation?"

When Rachel put it like that, Lionel began to fully understand what Monty had gone through to make the decision he had. The fact that he had clearly agonized over the decision gave Lionel pause. Maybe Monty did love him after all. His once-righteous indignation disintegrated.

"No, of course not. I would never expect him to sacrifice his brother's life to save my reputation." That begged the ultimate question, though.

"Who would do something like this?" Lionel mused out loud.

"Actually, I suspect Seamus O'Reilly had a hand in this."

"O'Reilly? Do you really think so?" Lionel thought for a moment. Of course, that made sense. Lionel's connection with Michael and Ian Stafford was very public—especially since the non-profit organization Ian and Megan had started for him had garnered a lot of publicity.

Damage to Lionel's reputation would not only harm Lionel, it would also taint the Staffords.

In addition to the financial hit they would take if his business went under, the drugging allegation would also do damage. Drugging was pervasive in the racing world and had come up sporadically in the dressage world as well. If Ian and Michael were closely associated with a twice-proven cheater, their reputations would be suspect as well. Both men's livelihoods and families would suffer substantially.

"Now that you know everything, you need to make things right with Monty. He told me that after the drug was discovered, he was planning to stand by you and support you. He would sacrifice his own career and finances to ensure you would be well and taken care of. He loves you, Lionel. I know you can see that."

Lionel's gaze softened as he looked back toward the stabling area where Monty would be waiting. His heart was still troubled, however.

"I'm not sure. He could be doing this just out of a sense of obligation to me. I want to hear it out of his own mouth before I believe it."

"Fine. Let's go see him and together we might be able to figure out another way out of this bad situation. You do remember that Ian Stafford and his friends are just a phone call away?"

"Of course! Rachel, you're a genius."

He offered his arm, and Rachel hooked hers through as they walked together back to the stabling area.

They found Monty in the same place they had left him. Monty cast Rachel a grateful glance, then looked at Lionel.

"Lionel, I know what I was planning to do is unforgivable, but can you at least understand why I felt I had no choice?"

Lionel spared a quick peek at Rachel, who smiled her encouragement. "Yes, Monty. Rachel explained in no uncertain terms that you really did not have a choice but to do everything you could to save your brother's life. I understand that now. She also told me that you were prepared to stand by me and support me once the bad news broke. Is that true?"

"Of course it's true. What else could I do? It would have been through my actions and my actions alone that you were implicated. I had to do what I could to make it right."

Lionel's heart sank. "So, it would be out of a sense of obligation and justice that you would do this?"

"Yes, that's it." Monty looked at Lionel, his confusion evident.

Instead of being comforted, in the wake of Monty's response, Lionel's expression changed from one of hope to one of hurt and loss.

"But you don't love me. Is that what you're trying to tell me?"

Lionel watched Monty's face for any reaction, hoping beyond hope that Monty would do something to either confirm or deny his assertion. He didn't have to wait long. Monty reached out and took Lionel in his arms.

At first, Lionel resisted the embrace, and kept his body stiff and unyielding, but when Monty didn't let him go, and began slowly rubbing his back in broad, soothing strokes, Lionel relented. Then it was as if the invisible dam that had been holding back every emotion Lionel had been experiencing since finding the syringe in Monty's possession broke. He began sobbing, and his body collapsed into Monty's arms. Both men held on to each other as if they would never let go.

"Of course I love you, you idiot," Monty softly chided his lover and pushed himself back far enough to be able to look into his eyes.

"I think I've loved you from the first moment I saw you. That's why we must find another way. Now that you know the truth, together we can figure out how to take this bastard down."

Lionel smiled through his tears and brushed back the pesky lock of hair that always seemed to fall onto Monty's brow. He then cradled Monty's face in his hand, holding it in place so he could gaze directly into his eyes.

"I'm glad I'm not the only one who fell in love at first sight. You are the first man I felt an attraction for since Nigel. The realization frightened me at first, because you're so young and vital. I'm old and stodgy. How could you find me attractive?"

Monty snorted his disagreement with that idea, and pulled himself abruptly from Lionel's embrace, holding him at arm's length, and scanning his body with a heated gaze.

"Old and stodgy? You've got to be kidding me. You're the most vital and energetic man I've ever met. When I asked Randall about you, and he told me your age, I didn't believe him. 'Old and stodgy,' my arse. I have a feeling that I will always be fighting to keep up with you well into our dotage."

"You expect us to be together that long, eh?" Lionel asked with a grin.

"Yes, and you know it," Monty replied. He drew Lionel close for a passionate kiss just to remind the man how he really felt about him. Then Rachel's amused voice interrupted their embrace, making them suddenly aware of their surroundings.

"Excuse me, boys, but while the two of you were busy reconciling, Beau was loaded, the lorry is closed up tight, and we are ready to go."

With a shared grin, the two men separated and followed Rachel to where their vehicles were parked and waiting.

Chapter 15

Lionel and Monty had driven separately in Lionel's car as they usually did for competitions in the EU, and before Rachel left them to take her usual place beside the lorry driver responsible for transporting Beau, Lionel stopped her and asked her to join him and Monty for their drive back. She readily agreed.

"I'm going to call Ian as soon as we get underway and start plotting how we're going to thwart O'Reilly, if it is indeed him behind this plot," Lionel told her as he gave Monty his phone. Monty quickly found Ian's number among Lionel's contacts and dialed. He then put the phone on speaker so they all could hear the conversation. After a couple of rings, Ian Stafford's voice came on the phone.

"Lionel, you bloody motherfucker, how have you been?" Lionel cast a chagrined look at Rachel, then gently cleared his throat, "Language, Ian. I've got you on speaker, and Rachel and Monty are here with me."

There was a moment of uncomfortable silence from the other end of the line, then Ian sheepishly responded, "Sorry, Rache, cheers, Monty. My apologies for the profanity."

Rachel laughed. "Not a problem, Ian. I've heard much worse around the stables. Most grooms don't take the time to censor their language. I'm used to it."

"Thanks, Rache, but still, I promise I'll behave. So, Lionel, to what do I owe the pleasure of this call?"

"Pleasure is far from it, Ian. I believe that Seamus O'Reilly may be up to his old tricks again."

"Tell me." Ian's tone instantly grew serious. Even over the phone Lionel could tell he now had the man's undivided attention.

Monty related the events as they had occurred to date, excluding only the aspects relating to Lionel's and his personal relationship.

"Bugger it!" Ian cursed. "It does sound like O'Reilly's work. I'll call Roger Davis right away and make sure your brother Gavin has around the clock protection immediately. I'll also have Roger check the backgrounds of every employee at the rehab facility. If O'Reilly believed he could drug Gavin at any time, he would have to have help from inside the facility."

Lionel shuddered at the possibility, and looked over at Monty, who was visibly pale at the thought that O'Reilly might have someone who worked in the facility his family trusted ready and willing to kill his brother.

At that point Rachel spoke up. "Is there anything we can do, Ian?"

"Monty should use the number the villain provided to call him and explain that since Beau was being moved today, the planting of the drug will have to wait until he's settled back home. That will stall his activities enough to give us time to put our resources in place. Does that sound all right to you?"

"Certainly," Monty said. "I'll call right away. He won't be happy, but there's nothing I can do. Beau's travel schedule is out of my control."

Their plan going forward solidified, Lionel hung up with Ian, and the trio stopped for petrol at a station along the motorway. Monty took that opportunity to place the call to O'Reilly's man. As anticipated, the man on the other end of the line wasn't pleased that the timeline had been delayed. Ultimately, however, he agreed that Monty would reconnect sometime tomorrow to let him know that he'd planted the drug.

Once he had hung up on the call to the mysterious man, Monty returned to the car to join the others. "I have a suspicion our man has someone working for him in our crew. The fact that he told me he had someone who would 'find' the illegal drug after I planted it makes that a distinct possibility, don't you think?"

Rachel sighed. "As much as I hate to admit it, you're probably right. I'll do an informal check of my folks to see if there's anyone that might be vulnerable to bribery or blackmail. Anyone in that situation would be easy to convince to help."

Lionel nodded. "I've been thinking about that too. It could be that O'Reilly's man convinced someone working for me that I've reverted to my old ways and doping again. It could be one explanation for Beau's extraordinary success. They might be thinking they're doing the right thing by exposing me."

"In any event," Rachel said, "I'll see what I can find."

Their plans having been made and finalized, the three settled back and tried to forget the turmoil that awaited them once they arrived back at Second Chance Farm.

Chapter 16

"So, what's the fucking hold up?"

Mickey Collins winced at the angry tone of Seamus' voice. He had just called him to tell him that Monty Campbell wouldn't be planting the illegal drug until tomorrow at the earliest.

"It couldn't be helped, boss." Mickey attempted to calm Seamus as he had on numerous occasions since he started working for the man over thirty years ago. "The horse is being transported, and there's no opportunity to leave the drug in a place it would certainly be found."

"You told me this was going to be done weeks ago. I knew I shouldn't have trusted you with something this complicated." Seamus was clearly agitated. Mickey knew along with his famously volatile temper, the man was suffering from high blood pressure and had been ignoring his doctors' warnings for years. He also smoked cigarettes constantly. Too much rage and excitement could push him over the edge to a heart attack or stroke. He tried once again to placate the man.

"Seamus, you have to trust me. Plans like this must work their way through on their own good time. You know this."

"I suppose you're right," Seamus said grudgingly. "Just make sure the bloody fag doesn't back out at the last minute. You have his brother under watch, and your man is ready to act on a moment's notice, right?"

Mickey sighed in irritation. Even after his years of service, the man didn't trust him?

"Of course. I have a man I trust in place as a counselor at the facility where Gavin Campbell is now living. You know it takes some time for a new employee to gain the trust of the management of a facility like this. After several weeks on the job, he now has full access to the patients. If

Monty Campbell decides to defy us and refuse to frame Lionel Hayes, our man will take his brother out quickly and efficiently."

"Good. Keep me posted."

Mickey hung up, then quickly disposed of the phone. Under normal circumstances, prison phone calls were routinely monitored and recorded, but Seamus' influence in the prison was such that Michael could smuggle a burner cell phone to Seamus without the guards raising a peep of objection. Nice arrangement, that.

Just to make sure his agent in the halfway house was still in place, Mickey used a different cell phone to place a call.

"Yes, boss. All is going to plan. There was a new visiting doctor that arrived today, but he appears to be here temporarily, and specifically to counsel the addicts that are closer to release."

"Good. Stay alert. I'll use this phone to give you the signal to implement our plan." He hung up and started pacing. Campbell should have called by now. What was keeping the man? Surely, he wouldn't sacrifice his brother to save a weakling like Lionel Hayes? Mickey decided to give the man another twenty-four hours, then he would contact his man at the farm to find out what was going on.

Chapter 17

The next morning dawned clear and sunny. Lionel had left Monty sleeping peacefully in the bedroom they now shared and was now walking down the aisle at Second Chance Farm, checking on the horses. He paused, as always, at Molly's stall to give the giant mare some much-appreciated attention.

"Hello, sweetheart. I've missed you." He stoked her forehead gently, then pulled a few sugar cubes out of his pocket and offered them to the mare, who gently lipped them from his hand. Molly was visibly pleased as she crunched the sugar in her huge jaws. As he continued petting the mare, his thoughts drifted to what had transpired since last night.

After they had arrived home right around midnight, Rachel saw to the process of unloading the lorry. She took responsibility for making sure Beau was comfortably bedded down and suffering no ill effects from the nearly eleven- hour drive from Switzerland. Confident that Rachel had everything under control, Lionel led Monty into his home, and straight to the master bedroom—the room he had once shared with Nigel—and in no uncertain terms told him he would be spending his nights here with Lionel from now on. Monty was speechless at Lionel's pronouncement.

The fact that he was asking Monty to take the place Nigel Crawford had occupied for several years before his death had clearly moved him. He finally spoke through what sounded like a lump in his throat.

"Are you sure, Lionel? I know how much Nigel meant to you, and that you loved him very much. I fear I will never be able to replace him."

Lionel had stepped closer to Monty and cradled his face in his hands. He looked deeply into his eyes.

"I'm very sure, Monty. I love you. Your place is here with me for as long as you want to be here. No, you are not Nigel, and I don't expect you to be. You're special in your own right." He sighed and looked in the direction of the bed in the center of the room.

"Truth be told, the love I had for Nigel was warm, comfortable, and safe. It was exactly what I needed at that time." His gaze returned to Monty, and he grinned mischievously. "What I feel for you is far from comfortable and safe, and I look forward to waking up next to you each morning for as long as you'll have me wondering what adventure we'll be pursing next."

"That will be forever, if I have anything to say about it," Monty replied, his voice choked with emotion. "I love you, darling, more than you can possibly know."

From that moment, although they were both exhausted, they shared a night of passionate lovemaking Lionel knew he would never forget. The morning, however, had found Lionel restless. This matter of O'Reilly and his evil plot weighed heavily on him. He had showered and dressed quietly, smiling to himself as he did so, because through it all, Monty didn't move an inch. The man was clearly worn out both physically and emotionally after everything that had transpired in the last 48 hours.

The phone in his back jeans pocket vibrated, and he took it out. It was Ian. His mood immediately sobered.

"Ian," he said, "thank you for calling. Have you learned anything?"

"We have. Roger was able to determine that one of the counselors at the facility is relatively new, and of Irish descent. Roger did a background check and discovered that the man has records only going back about five years. Before that, he doesn't appear to exist. He's certain that's our man. Since the discovery, Roger sent an operative in posing as a doctor. He's keeping an eye on the man and will keep Gavin safe."

"That's great news, Ian. What about the rest?"

"I've been waiting to hear from Rachel, but unfortunately, all Roger can find on your employees at Second Chance is that one is a pretty serious animal rights activist. He's on numerous online organizations that champion animal rights. His name is Rex Allenson. Do you know the man?"

"Of course I do. He's one of my hardest workers, and he shows genuine concern for the horses." Lionel thought for a moment. "Now that you mention it, though, he has been casting nasty looks my way when he thought I wasn't looking. He could be someone O'Reilly might use—especially if he convinced the man I was playing dirty. He wouldn't condone drugging any of the horses. That would be tantamount to abuse in his eyes."

"That's good to know. Since Monty destroyed the vial of banned substance, there's no danger of you being caught 'red handed' doing anything wrong but knowing the identity of the person tasked with trumpeting your guilt may come in handy."

"Agreed."

Chapter 18

Lionel was just finishing his rounds in the stable when Monty appeared. "Good morning!" Lionel greeted Monty with a hug and a kiss on the cheek. Monty gave him a confused look, clearly expecting more from Lionel than a chaste hug and kiss after last night, but Lionel quickly explained his behavior. He related Rachel's discovery of Lionel and Nigel in a compromising position all those years ago and explained that he and Nigel had made it a point not to display their affections quite so obviously when in the more public areas of the stable.

Monty grinned and agreed with Lionel's approach. "Rachel walked in on you, eh? That must have been an interesting conversation."

"Yes, well, she didn't know we were gay, and actually had developed a sort of crush on me," Lionel sheepishly explained.

Monty's grin got even bigger. "Oh, my God, Lionel, how did she react?"

"I think she was more embarrassed than anything. I know Nigel and I were mortified. We resolved to behave more circumspectly from that day forward."

"A good policy. I'm glad you explained. I was a bit worried I'd done something wrong."

It was now Lionel's turn to grin. "Not at all, sweetheart. You were fabulous, and you know it."

Monty's answering grin suddenly disappeared when he noticed Rex Allenson watching them from the other end of the aisle.

"Rex, is there something we can do for you?" he asked, in effect calling Rex out for plainly eavesdropping on their conversation.

"No, sir. Nothing at all. Sorry." The man hurriedly found a muck rake and bucket and began cleaning the nearest stall. Lionel took

Monty by the arm and led him to the tack room at the end of the aisle. The two entered, then Lionel closed the door.

"That reminds me. Ian just called and told me that O'Reilly does have a man working at the facility your brother is in."

Monty instantly paled. "My God, Lionel. We've got to get Gavin out of there. He's in danger. It's only a matter of time before O'Reilly's man realizes I'm not going to plant the drug."

Lionel placed a hand on Monty's shoulder and squeezed gently. "Easy, love. Ian's friend Roger Davis has a man in place at the facility posing as a doctor to keep an eye on the man. Matters are under control."

Monty didn't seem appeased. "I don't know, Lionel. I trust Ian, but O'Reilly is powerful and may have connections his friend may not know about. I want to go up there and bring Gavin back here so he's safe."

A cold hand wrapped around his heart as Lionel contemplated Monty confronting one of Seamus O'Reilly's killers. There was no way he would allow Monty to place himself in danger. "No, Monty. I forbid it. You're not going."

Monty's expression immediately contorted into an angry glare in response to Lionel's imperious tone. "Just try to stop me, Lionel. I love my brother, and if there's something I can do to remove him from a life-threatening situation, I'll do it in a heartbeat. You have a choice. You can come with me, or you can stay here and wait for me to return with Gavin."

Lionel knew in that moment that there was no way he would allow Monty to travel to London by himself. "All right, I'm coming with you. Let's go now. I'll call Ian and let him know what's happening."

"No. Lionel, please don't tell Ian. He might try to stop me, and I can't let that happen."

Lionel hesitated. Every part of his being told him that he needed to tell Ian that he and Monty were on their way to the facility in London to remove Gavin from danger, but Monty appeared adamant that he not. He did agree that it was quite possible that Ian would try to stop Monty from intervening, but in his own mind, that wasn't a bad thing. Ultimately, though, Lionel decided not to betray Monty's trust, and he did not call Ian.

Chapter 19

It had been twenty-four hours since his last contact with his man at Second Chance Farm, and Mickey was done waiting. Either the man had failed in his responsibilities, or he had to assume Monty Campbell wasn't going to honor his promise to plant the illegal drug.

"Yes, sir." The man answered his phone on the second ring. "I just looked in the medical supplies like you told me, and there isn't anything that looks illegal in here. Just the normal ointments and bandages you might see in any other horse's medical supplies."

"Is Mr. Hayes anywhere close by? What about his Scottish friend? Is he there in the stables?"

"No sir. In fact, both the Scot and Mr. Hayes left a few minutes ago. Drove away in a rush, actually. I'm not sure where they were going."

Mickey cursed. "I think I might have an idea." *Yes, a very good idea.* He turned his attention back to the man on the phone. "It appears I may have been mistaken about Mr. Hayes. I appreciate your dedication, however."

"No problem, sir. But if I may say so, I'm glad Mr. Hayes hasn't gone back to cheating. He's a good man and treats all his horses well."

Mickey struggled to keep the revulsion he was feeling at the excessive niceness of the man out of his voice. "Yes, well, there is that. Goodbye." Mickey quickly hung up the phone and contacted his man at the halfway house in London.

"It appears your services will be needed after all. You have my order. Kill Gavin Campbell and be sure to make it look like an overdose."

"Consider it done," the man on the other end of the line responded, his voice cold, without emotion.

Mickey hung up the phone, and a feeling of dread overtook him. Strange, as matters stood, he should be feeling quite smug right now, but his instincts were telling him something was wrong. Never one to discount his gut, which had saved his life on more than one occasion, he decided to go to the halfway house himself to make sure his orders were carried out. Not only that, Mickey arranged with one of his associates to get him another syringe of heroin laced with fentanyl. One could never take any chances when the objective was this important.

IT SEEMED TO MONTY that he and Lionel had been on the road forever when the street signs for London started appearing on the M23 motorway. They were approaching the halfway house address when Monty spotted several police vehicles, their lights flashing, just outside.

Monty's heart rate accelerated the closer they got to the halfway house. He gripped the dashboard with his left hand, and Lionel's forearm with his right. "My God, Lionel, hurry. We might be too late."

To his credit, Lionel patiently maneuvered the car as close as he could to the scene. As soon as the car was parked, Monty sprang from the vehicle Lionel following closely behind. Just as they approached one of the constables on scene, they saw two uniformed officers leave the building, firmly holding a man in handcuffs between them.

Monty addressed the policeman who appeared to be in charge. "Officer, I'm Monty Campbell. My brother Gavin is a resident here. I have reason to believe he may be in danger."

"Ah, yes. Mr. Campbell. I believe there is someone here looking for you." The man indicated a gentleman in a button-down dress shirt and Dockers slacks speaking casually with another plainclothes officer. As if sensing their presence, the man turned toward Monty and Lionel as they approached. Lionel gasped when he noticed the man's face was bruised, and he had a bleeding cut over one eye. When the man reached out to shake Monty's hand, Lionel noticed his knuckles were bruised and bloody as well.

"Mr. Campbell, hello. I'm Andrew Cross. I work for Davis Security and was placed here to keep watch over your brother Gavin." The man indicated the prisoner as he was placed in the back seat of a police car. "As you can see, and as we anticipated, this man tried to kill Gavin with a syringe of heroin laced with fentanyl. I was able to stop him before he did the deed."

Monty indicated Andrew's face with a grimace. "It appears he wasn't about to go quietly."

Cross chuckled his agreement. "It did take some persuasion to convince him not to go through with it." He worked his jaw in an obvious attempt to reset it in place. Monty noticed another bruise beginning to form there.

Lionel had been listening in. "Thank God you prevailed." He reached out to shake the man's hand as well. "I'm Lionel Hayes, Mr. Cross."

"Ah, yes, Mr. Hayes. Ian Stafford sends his best." He then turned back to Monty. "Your brother is just inside. He's a bit shaken, but otherwise OK. I'm certain he'll be happy to see you."

Cross hadn't even finished that sentence before Monty was bounding up the stairs to the entrance to the facility. As he entered, it took a moment for his eyes to adjust from the difference between the bright sun outside and the shadows of the building interior. Then he heard his name come from off to his right. The owner of the voice was not at all happy to see him.

"Monty. What the hell is going on here? They told me someone tried to kill me. Is this your doing?"

Monty knew he had plenty of explaining to do, and not much time within which to do it. It didn't help that the area was crawling with police and crime scene investigators, who appeared to be taking a great deal of interest in their conversation. He spotted an empty office near the corridor in which they were standing, and gently tried to lead his brother in that direction.

"Gavin, if you just give me a couple of minutes, I can explain everything."

Thankfully, Gavin allowed himself to be directed into the office, and Monty quietly closed the door behind him. Just before the door was completely closed, Monty looked up to see Lionel standing in the corridor. He gave his lover a thumbs-up gesture, and tried to smile, but knew he failed miserably. Lionel said nothing but moved his right hand over his heart to show his love and support. Gavin fought back the tears that threatened to fall, then nodded his acknowledgment and thanks, then shut the door.

Although Monty motioned that his brother should sit, Gavin began pacing the room, unable to contain the nervous energy that today's events had generated.

"So, is it true that some thug just tried to kill me, and that the only thing that saved me was the fact that you knew it was going to happen and sent someone to stop it?"

"Well, yes. That's true, but before you jump to any more conclusions, give me a minute to tell you the whole story."

Gavin smiled sarcastically. "Oh, by all means tell me the story. I'm sure I'll enjoy it immensely."

"I will, but first, stop that infernal pacing. It's making me crazy. Just sit for a few minutes while I tell you this, all right?"

Gavin grunted his dissatisfaction but did manage to sit in one of the office chairs. "All right. I'm all ears. Tell me."

Monty proceeded to tell Gavin everything that had happened since the day the unknown man had called him in his hotel room in Lausanne and threatened him, with the exception of his private moments with Lionel. Those were not his to share and didn't have any real bearing on the story. He did make it clear to Gavin that he and Lionel had become more than just trainer and client.

Gavin, to his credit, allowed Monty to speak without interruption. When he finished, Gavin appeared thoughtful.

"So, do you think the danger has passed?"

Monty had the grace to look uncomfortable. "No, I don't. If the man behind this plot is Seamus O'Reilly, he won't stop until Lionel is harmed in some way. He may even persist in wanting you dead to take his revenge on me as well. Lionel and I would like you to come to Hickstead with us and stay at the farm until Ian Stafford and his friends can find O'Reilly's agent on the outside. Until that happens, I think you're still in danger, as is Lionel."

Gavin considered for a moment. "All right, I'll come with you." He then got a bit of a mischievous grin on his face. "I'd definitely like to meet Lionel. I'd like to shake the hand of the man that caught my brother's wandering eye."

Monty frowned, then punched Gavin in the arm with a bit more force than necessary. "You'll say nothing of my 'wandering eye.' That behavior is in the past. My relationship with Lionel is the real thing, and I'll not have you ruin it by dredging up the past."

"Ow, that hurt!" Gavin complained, rubbing the spot that would probably bear a bruise. "All right, I'll be good. Just get me out of this place."

Monty opened the office door, and he and Gavin joined Lionel in the corridor. None of them noticed that one of the constables was watching them with more than just idle interest.

Chapter 20

Mickey watched Lionel and Monty lead Gavin from the house and take him toward Lionel's car. He reached into the coat pocket of the constable's uniform he kept at his flat for just such an occasion. The uniform had frequently made it possible to walk around crime scenes, planting or lifting evidence as O'Reilly saw fit. He fingered the syringe and pondered his next move.

As he observed Lionel and Monty interact at the halfway house, he realized that they were a couple, and in love. There was something about their easy manner with each other, Gavin's instant acceptance of the two as a couple, and their easy camaraderie that made Mickey's blood boil.

How dare they be so happy, so content with life when I'm trapped in a life of literal servitude to a man who couldn't care less whether I'm happy or not as long as I blindly followed the man's orders. Looking back over the life he had lived at the beck and call of Seamus O'Reilly, Mickey felt nothing but rage. Over thirty years of loyalty pledging his life and service to a man who even now questioned his every decision and what did he have? A future spent living in the shadows with nothing to show for it but a miniscule bank account and a boss who could order his death at the slightest infraction. In this case, the fact that his plan to blackmail Monty Campbell had backfired spectacularly made Mickey certain he had signed his own death warrant.

At that moment, something within Mickey Collins snapped. He no longer cared about Seamus' grand plan for revenge. Mickey was out for revenge for himself. If Monty Campbell had just followed directions, Seamus's lust for revenge would have been satisfied, and

Mickey's life wouldn't be in jeopardy. He resolved in that moment that Monty Campbell would have to die.

Mickey removed the syringe from its pouch slowly approached the men from behind. When he was close enough to deliver the fatal injection, he exposed the syringe and moved toward Monty with deadly purpose. Just as he was about to stick Monty in the shoulder, Lionel looked up and saw him.

It only took a fraction of a second for Lionel to understand what was about to happen. He screamed, "Monty, watch out!"

Lionel knew in that moment that nothing and no one would take away the man he loved. Nigel's death had been out of his control, and he had suffered with that knowledge for years before he found peace. Now, there was something he could do to prevent his lover's death and was damn sure going to do it. Before anyone could intervene, Lionel pushed Monty out of the way and placed his body between Monty and the deadly syringe.

At the same time, hands were grasping Mickey by the shoulders and pulling him back, but not before he was able to stick the needle into Lionel's upper arm. He started pushing the plunger down but didn't complete the motion before he was wrestled to the ground.

Lionel had fallen to the ground, and although not all the drug had reached his system, enough had penetrated to be causing effects. Monty noticed immediately. He began shouting to be heard over the commotion caused by Mickey's sudden attack.

"Someone get some Narcan here, now. I know you have it. He needs it right away or he'll die." He looked at Lionel, who was starting to lose consciousness. "Lionel, stay with me. We're getting you help. You're going to be fine."

Lionel smiled weakly, the drug taking effect quickly. "So glad you're all right Monty. I couldn't let him take you from me. I love you."

"I love you, too, you stupid man." At that point, a doctor from the halfway house arrived with an injectable dose of Narcan. He administered it immediately, and Lionel quickly snapped back to full awareness.

Meanwhile, the constables had identified Mickey Collins by scanning his fingerprints and were taking him into custody.

"You gents might as well shoot me now and get it over with," Mickey groaned to the police. "Once my boss finds out I didn't honor my promise, my life won't be worth a tinker's damn."

"And who might that boss be, you bloody bastard?"

In that moment, Mickey knew only that it was his life or Seamus' in the balance. Certain that once Seamus found out Mickey had failed, he would order his death, Mickey did what any man would do to save himself. "It was Seamus O'Reilly who hired me to do the job. If you protect me, I'll testify to as much in court."

Later that evening, when Seamus learned that Mickey had failed, that Lionel Hayes was safe, Ian Stafford still thrived, and Mickey had turned state's evidence against him, Seamus massive temper exploded. Unfortunately for him, the tremendous stress his temper levelled on his heart was too much for it to take. He died in his cell instantly of a massive heart attack.

Epilogue

This year's World Cup competition in Rome had drawn a massive audience, and even the equestrian events had been sold out weeks in advance. It was common knowledge within the close-knit British equestrian community that the winners of this year's World Cup competition would establish themselves as the favorites for next year's Olympic Games in Tokyo.

This evening, after the open competition yesterday, there were five remaining horses in medal contention. Gideon's Rainbow, ridden by Monty Campbell and owned by Lionel Hayes, representing Great Britain, was the crowd favorite.

Beau, with Monty astride, was waiting patiently for the stewards to replace a couple of downed poles left by the rider before them, and Lionel stood at his head, stroking his neck. Appearances would suggest Lionel was trying to calm his horse, but in truth, it was the horse's calm demeanor that was helping Lionel stay on an even keel.

Monty looked up into the audience, found his parents and Gavin then grinned, nodding in greeting. They waved enthusiastically in return. Monty spared a moment to reflect on the events of the past several months. Gavin had come to live with Lionel and Monty at Second Chance Farm, and ended up being a Godsend to Rachel, who found plenty of chores around the farm to keep him busy. Monty smiled to himself. If he wasn't mistaken, there might be something growing between Rachel and Gavin. He had caught each of them looking somewhat longingly at the other when the other wasn't looking.

Monty and Lionel had even teased Rachel about her cougar tendencies. After all, Gavin had just turned twenty- two, and Rachel was twenty-eight. Rachel had blushed furiously at the implications, but she also reminded Monty that Gavin's life experiences had matured him way beyond his years. Monty knew she was right. Gavin was much more mature that Monty himself had been at that age, and his experiences as a recovering addict had matured him. He made of point of telling Gavin as often as possible how proud he was of him.

Returning his thoughts to the present, Monty watched as Lionel also scanned the crowd and found Michael and Jessica and Ian and Megan Stafford sitting with Monty's family. Lionel smiled a greeting as well, although his smile was tense.

Monty leaned down and whispered softly to Lionel. "Don't worry, love. Beau and I have done this a million times. We've got this."

Lionel looked up at the man he loved with his whole heart and sighed. "Deep down, I know that, but this is the World Cup, Monty. You can't possibly blame me for being nervous."

Rachel approached from the stabling area with a cooler slung over her arm. "We're close to time, Monty. Good luck."

Monty gathered the reins and clucked softly to Beau. "All right, old man. It's your turn to go. Let's show them how it's done, shall we?"

As if he understood every word, Beau snorted and nodded vigorously. He was ready to go.

The three humans laughed at the horse's antics, then Beau and Monty went off. True to form, Monty and Beau performed their round perfectly and earned themselves an individual gold medal. Later that evening, after Monty had received his medal, and the crowds started to disburse, he found Lionel and dragged him to an isolated corner of the stabling area.

"I've been waiting to do this all day," Monty groaned as he covered Lionel's mouth with his in a passionate kiss.

Lionel responded with a passion all his own, and it didn't take long for Monty to start looking for an empty stall where they could have some privacy.

Lionel stopped him. "No, love. We can't do this now. There are members of the press wandering around looking for you to get an interview. The last thing we need is someone catching us shagging like rabbits in an empty stall."

Monty's ardor cooled at the mental image Lionel had created. He sighed. "You're right, love. But just wait until I get you back to our room. You will be the happiest man in the world before the night is over."

Lionel grinned. "I am already the happiest man in the world, thanks to you. Now let's go get your interviews over with so we can be alone."

"Your wish is my command, my lord." Monty mockingly bowed.

Just then, Beau, who had been watching the two men with interest from his stall nearby, neighed loudly.

Lionel laughed. "I think he can understand us."

Monty laughed as well. "I know he can, and I'm glad he can't talk. He definitely knows too much."

Each man gave Beau a crisp, red, apple, then they headed toward the press area. Beau watched the men go, and when they were finally out of sight, he nodded his approval.

Also from **Kimberly Beckett**
DRESSAGE DREAMING

Michael Stafford was on top of the world. A proud member of the British Olympic Dressage Team and Olympic gold medalist, his life was perfect. Then, he lost his mount, his fiancée left him for another man, and now his brother has been arrested for manslaughter. He believes his luck has turned when he learns that a beautiful and talented stallion is available in Germany, just in time to compete in the next World Cup competition. The horse's name is Tempest.

Jessica Warren is an up and coming American dressage prodigy with a brilliant future. Orphaned at the age of 21 when her parents were tragically killed in a car accident and the legal guardian of her younger sister, Jessica has lost her competition mount to injury and needs a new horse if she wants to compete in next year's World Cup. She learns of a spectacular horse available in Germany named Tempest, but when Jessica arrives in Germany with her trainer, she discovers she will have to compete with the extremely handsome and talented Michael Stafford for the right to ride Tempest. Jessica has nothing but respect for Michael, but sparks fly when they're thrown together in a competition that both must win. Who will win Tempest? Will Michael be able to trust another woman with his heart? Will Jessica allow herself to be loved, or will her personal demons keep them apart?

Available on Amazon: **DRESSAGE DREAMING**

RACING TOWARD LOVE

IAN STAFFORD IS A FORMER British Special Forces soldier and Afghanistan war veteran who still has nightmares after watching his best friend cut down by a sniper in a remote village in Afghanistan. When he sees a woman in a local pub being harassed and threatened, he intervenes. During the ensuing brawl, the woman escapes, but Ian accidentally stabs one of his attackers who later dies. Ian is charged with manslaughter, and the woman who can exonerate him has disappeared.

Megan Brady and her father Daniel never imagined that the thoroughbred colt they raised from birth would grow up to be a contender for the British Triple Crown. Seabiscuit II is the last horse you might imagine as a champion if judged by looks alone. Like his namesake, Seabiscuit II is not much to look at, but has a heart as big as all outdoors, and refuses to be beaten. Unfortunately, the Irish mob has also taken notice and has approached Megan's brother Stephen with an offer of a bribe to purposely lose the most important race of his career. Stephen refused, and Megan has taken it upon herself to thwart the mob, but their brutal tactics nearly see her raped until Ian steps in to save her. Megan knows she must come out of hiding to exonerate Ian, but knows if she does, the mob will be there too. Meanwhile the date of the big race approaches.

Available on Amazon: **RACING TOWARD LOVE**

Can Megan's example of courage in the face of overwhelming odds, and the will to prevail even when the going looks tough, help Ian come to grips with his grief, and give him the courage to forgive himself and allow himself to live and love again? Will Ian be able to trust Megan with his heart?

About the Author

Ever since she can remember, Kimberly Beckett has loved horses. She wore out 4 rocking horses before she was 5 years old, and as she got older, she read every horse story in print, from *Black Beauty* to *My Friend Flicka*. It wasn't until she got her first job as an attorney for the federal government, however, that could afford to buy her first horse, and she hasn't been without at least one ever since.

She has been riding dressage for several years and has earned her United States Dressage Federation Bronze Medal. When she wasn't reading about horses, she was reading romance novels, and her favorites always involve an alpha male Hero riding a magnificent horse. Kimberly has now found a way to combine her love of horses with her love of romance by writing her own version of equine-facilitated happily ever afters. She truly believes that Horses Heal Hearts. She lives in southwest Ohio with her two adopted greyhounds, and two warmblood horses.

If you loved *Lionel's Leap of Faith,* please read the other books in Kimberly's Horses Heal Hearts Series, Dressage Dreaming, where readers are first introduced to Ian Stafford, his brother, Michael, and Michael's love, Jessica Warren; Racing Toward Love, which is where we first meet Michael's brother, Ian Stafford; Her Forever Love, which tells the story of Jessica's dressage trainer, Liz Randall, and her second chance at love; and Winning Hailey's Heart, Jessica;s sister Hailey's love story.

To find out more about Kimberly, and to keep up with her next release, please visit her website, www.kimberlybeckett.com and sign up for her periodic email updates.

Also by Kimberly Beckett

Horses Heal Hearts
Dressage Dreaming
Racing Toward Love
Lionel's Leap of Faith
Her Forever Love
Winning Hailey's Heart

Watch for more at https://www.kimberlybeckett.com.

About the Author

Ever since she can remember, Kimberly Beckett has loved horses. She wore out 4 rocking horses before she was 5 years old, and as she got older, she read every horse story in print, from *Black Beauty* to *My Friend Flicka*. It wasn't until she got her first job as an attorney for the federal government, however, that could afford to buy her first horse, and she hasn't been without at least one ever since. She has been riding dressage for several years and has earned her United States Dressage Federation Bronze Medal. When she wasn't reading about horses, she was reading romance novels, and her favorites always involved an alpha male Hero riding a magnificent horse. Kimberly has now found a way to combine her love of horses with her love of romance by writing her own version of equine-facilitated happily ever afters. She truly believes that Horses Heal Hearts. She lives in southwest Ohio with her two adopted greyhounds, and two warmblood horses.

If you loved *Racing Toward Love*, please read the first book in Kimberly's Horses Heal Hearts Series, Dressage Dreaming, where readers are first introduced to Ian Stafford, his brother, Michael, and Michael's love, Jessica Warren.

To find out more about Kimberly, and to keep up with her next release, please visit her website and sign up for her periodic email updates.

Read more at https://www.kimberlybeckett.com.

www.ingramcontent.com/pod-product-compliance
Lightning Source LLC
Chambersburg PA
CBHW021233130726
47988CB00002B/951